TALKS TO THE WIND

Talks to the Wind

By

Joe Wodatch Sr.

This one is dedicated to you

TALKS TO THE WIND

PREFACE

The voices in my head have returned to remind me that I am not finished yet, there are still things to be told and people that need to know. I presume they are right and will attempt to slow down the fast paced thoughts and be precise.

Come with me, back to the Adirondack Mountains and feel the wonder and beauty of the real wilderness. I don't mean the towns or lakes and rivers you see by the roadways; I mean the real wilderness of the back country. The places where the animals don't know what you are. Where the chickadees land on you and chirp because they have no fear. The place of Monarch butterflies that are scarce elsewhere, still blossom here. To smell clean mountain air with no hint of fumes and feel a gentle breeze filled with the fragrance of true forest. Walk through the tall ferns next to rapid brooks and let the sound sooth your weariness. This is how it's meant to be, not tucked away in a house or car. I know an old man whose lived his entire life out here and have never met someone so at peace. It was not a hard choice to live this way, but I needed someone to share it with. I have had that, and now I have returned alone to live as the old man did and this place has kept its promise and so must I to tell the tale

While I live out here in isolation I am not alone. Mother Nature has given me plenty of company with life of all sorts all around me and I swear they understand me when I talk with them. Being totally away from distractions my brain cleans itself and I become more aware of things around me. Do I worry about getting hurt or killed? No, that is out of my control; I'm careful and make sure of my surroundings. I am learning to read the terrain so as not to get lost. I've made costly mistakes when younger and hopeful I learned from them.

So back to the path and story I return. It is 2016 and though the age of technology is upon us there is no such thing out here, only an awareness of its existence. Good or bad is yet to be seen, and there good arguments for both sides. Steven Hawkins seems to have thoughts about it, and I value his input as I do anyone with exceptional intelligent thought. I live and see things much different than most and whether that is good or bad is yet to be found out. I'd better turn this back into an actual tale before the reader gets too bored.

Chapter One

The doe I was feeding startled suddenly; her ears turning as she sniffed the air. She bolted and bounded away to my left. I listened but heard nothing and I too smelled the air, again nothing. Moments later, very faintly I heard voices far away but clear in the quietness of this place. I crept into thicker brush and waited wondering who would be this far into this wild country.

In a short while a woman stumbled close to where I was. She was talking to herself or to her surrounding, I couldn't tell which. She appeared to be in her early to mid thirties with long red hair flowing from beneath her hat. She wore jeans and hiking boots and a red and black plaid shirt with a small pack of some sort thrown over her left shoulder. As she approach closer I realized she was talking to her surroundings. I crouched lower so as not to be seen,

Because I was naked except for my jeans, barefoot and shirtless might be too much for her. She stopped just a few yards away and looked in my direction. "You can come out, I don't bite". She called.

I stood and stepped out of the brush, and she smiled.

"No need to be afraid, I knew you was nearby, and that's why I started talking. Sorry about scaring the deer though."

"Who are you and how did you get here?" I said softly so the questions wouldn't sound angry.

"I walked, and searched. I've been out here for days looking to see if the story was true that there was a man living out here. And low and behold here you are, and my name is Anna."

"Why try to find me? I asked as I stepped closer. She had green eyes and was quiet attractive.

"I had to know if you were real or rumor. The idea of living out here like you do has been a fantasy of mine since I was a young teen. I thought we might share some ideas." With that she removed the pack from her shoulder and sat on the damp forest floor. I sat a few feet away and leaned on a downed tree to look relaxed. I wasn't, my heart raced with thoughts that I could be found so easy. I forgot that I had no reason to hide. "Are you camped far from here?"

"Not really, I kept moving except at night I slept on the ground under whatever shelter I could find."

"Weren't you afraid of bears or something?"

"No, I don't bother them they don't bother me. Mutual respect I think it's called."

Lord she really does think like me, I said to myself.

"I notice you don't have any scratches for someone walking shirtless in thick brush and no insect bites either."

I chuckled "mutual respect." And she laughed laughter of gaiety that was pleasant to hear. "And now that you've found me; what do we do next?"

TALKS TO THE WIND

"Perhaps if you don't mind, I'll join you for awhile and see what develops. Please don't say no, I've come quite a long way to be rejected."

"How could I say no to some companionship for awhile? You're pleasant to look at plus I've missed human conversation even though I shouldn't admit that. The few people I've talked with don't understand me. You on the other hand just might."

"What direction shall we go?" She stood as she asked.

"Southeast." I answered pointing. "There's a place I'd like you to see."

Conversation was light as they walked through rough terrain and finally arrived by Rock Pond. "This end is shallow with a sandy bottom if you want to freshen up. There's a small camp not far from here."

"No thanks, I'm doing just fine. It is pretty with the sky reflecting on the water like a mirror. The water is so still without even a ripple. I'll clean up later."

"I didn't mean anything." I stammered, "It's not like I meant skinny dipping or something."

She laughed, "I know what you meant and it's alright." She pointed to where a small brook fed the pond. "Can we go over there?"

Moments later they sat on boulders where the brook and pond met. She removed her boots rolled her jeans to her knees and placed her feet in the water. "My God it's cold!"

"Most of the fast water around here is because its spring fed." He stood in the stream next to her wet to his knees

"Do you come here often?"

"Not really; I move around a lot with the urge to find new wonders. I have places where I spend more time and one of them is not far from here. It's a small log cabin that's been deserted for many years. It's right on a lake which surprises me that nobody goes there."

"Is that where we're headed?"

"Maybe, it's up to you. I found a really great place I want you to see but it's too far to walk in one day."

"Then the cabin on the lake it is."

Within an hour and a half, he had her standing on the shore of the lake across from them was the rundown log cabin he spoke of. It sat nestled beneath tall pines on a point of land jutting into a bay of the lake. "It doesn't look like much but I keep canned goods in the cupboards and there is a fireplace to cook with."

Moments later Anna opened the door looked inside and said "Neat, I like it." She took note that there were only two rooms. Where she stood, were the fireplace and a table and bench by the window. In the other room were two bunk beds a small table with a kerosene lamp and a smaller window between the two beds.

"You start a fire and I'll cook supper." She said as she looked in the cupboards. "Beans or stew?" she asked.

As they finished supper he said "I can hang a partition between the beds or I can move a bed out here in this room."

"Neither one, it's fine as is. Stop worrying about me; I'm not the shy one."

He smiled, "I haven't had much female company for a long time that's all."

She laughed at that, "remember I told you I don't bite."

Later as they stood outside watching the sun set over the water she said quietly, "I'm what you see, nothing more nothing less, no secrets and no baggage. I love the outdoors and nature more than most people so when I heard about you, I had to learn more."

"Why would anyone be talking about me, I don't know that many people and it's rare I go anywhere near town."

"In this age of technology rumors spread about some hermit who talks to animals and lives like one of them. At first sight of you I knew they were wrong. I think I expected a breaded wild looking person with a deranged appearance but I had to find out." She smiled, "You're more like I was hoping for and you're handsome."

"Thanks." He said softly "I don't get many compliments. Appearances don't matter much out here. At least they didn't." he added.

"Can you yell and have animals come to your rescue, like Tarzan?"

He really had to laugh at that one. "No but the animals do warn me if something's wrong, like the doe I was feeding this morning." Then he thought for a minute about the reference to Tarzan. "I don't usually go shirtless. Barefoot yes, but the weather has been so glorious lately, I was taking advantage of it."

It was Anna's turn to smile. "We've been together for most of the day and you haven't told me what I should call you."

"Joe, I'm sorry I should have said when you told me yours. It didn't occur to me because what's a name out here."

"Shall we retire?"

"Sounds like a great idea; we have a long trek in the morning."

Later that night he heard her get up and go into the other room. He heard splashing outside but he didn't hear the door open or close so he went to investigate. She stood by the window watching intently.

"Are you alright?"

She jumped at the sound of his voice, and then laughed. "I heard something by the door. Just a pair of otters playing. Go back to bed and I'll be in shortly."

Joe did as he was told laughing to himself. He hadn't been told what do in many years. He heard Anna come in a short time later and slip into her sleeping bag.

"Are you awake?" she whispered.

"Yes, and I didn't mean to startle you before. I'm a light sleeper."

"And I didn't mean to order you back to bed either. I think we both need to make slight adjustments for one another."

"Fair enough, sleep well."

"You too, I'll try not disturb you again."

They woke with the smell of pine in their nostrils and bright sun creeping through the cracks in the log walls. Joe stood, stretched and pulled on his jeans, walked to the outhouse and then knelt by the water and splashed his head and saw Anna headed for the outhouse. He went inside to stir the coals in the fireplace. It was time for coffee. She came in moments later to find a pot next to the fire just beginning to perk. "You look rested, I mean you look nice." She had changed her plaid shirt for a lighter pale green shirt and traded her jeans for tan slacks. Now she wore sneakers instead of boots.

She knew he was giving her the once over look and responded with, "I'm not ready for bare feet yet and I only have a couple changes of clothes. I didn't know how long I'd be out here."

"Please stay." He blurted out. "I mean you stay as long as you like. I'll put on a shirt, I have one in back. Joe went into the bedroom and returned wearing a deep blue long sleeved shirt.

"Would you wear that if I wasn't here?"

"Maybe, let's have some coffee, you do drink coffee?"

"Of course. Where are we headed today?"

"To meet a friend of mind, his approval of you is important to me."

She frowned slightly and looked nervous but said nothing.

Within an hour of hiking Joe stopped suddenly, and gave a short whistle, waited and whistled again. Seconds later Ranger came loping toward them. Joe knelt and Ranger climbed to his shoulder. Joe stood turned toward Anna and bowed ever so slightly. "This is Anna."

She stepped closer and reached out to pat his furry head. Ranger smelled her fingers then put his head down. She patted him and smiled. "This is your friend whose approval you needed."

"You passed with flying colors, he would not have approached if you presented anything but what you are. And to let you touch him was more than I could have hope for. He has been my only companion for a long time." Joe gave her a big smile. "Welcome to my world."

"I've never been tested by an animal before."

"This wasn't a test; I just wanted you two to meet. No more jokes I promise. It was funny through, the way you looked when I said I wanted you to meet someone."

They began to walk slower and deeper into forest, Ranger riding on Joe's shoulder, Anna right beside them. It was a very pleasant walk, with birds singing in the distance abundance of wildlife to watch and the fragrance of wild flowers. They stopped several times to rest and talk pleasantly. They laughed at the thought of two strangers getting along together so well. It became more relaxed for them both.

TALKS TO THE WIND

Chapter Two

They arrived by New Pond just before dusk and decided to stay there for the night. After a light meal they rolled out their sleeping bags, put them next to the small fire. Joe smiled because hers was next to his and not on the other side of the fire. "Some creatures might come by during the night but they won't bother us." He said "Most are just curious and will continue on their way."

Sleep came quickly because of the long trek they did that day most of which was mountains.

Morning came with overcast sky and the threat of rain. After their coffee they headed south east again. The walking was easy with little underbrush to bar their way. They had only gone a couple of miles before the rain started. Anna had a hood poncho and Joe didn't mind the rain so they continued for a mile or two more before stopping. They stood under a huge fir tree for shelter from the downpour.

"Are you all right?" Anna asked, "You're soaked."

"I needed a shower anyway. Besides you get used to it after awhile."

"You look miserable and you're shivering, that's not good."

"You want a fire? I'll try to start one."

"I don't need it but you look as though you could use it."

"No, we'll keep moving; there's another hunters shack a little further on. We'll use that to get warm." Within half an hour, they had a small fire going in a woodstove. Joe stripped his wet clothes hung them near the fire while Anna threw her sleeping bag over his shoulders. "I guess the shyness is over," he joked while still shivering a little.

"What do you do if you need medical help?"

"I don't think much about that because I never or hardly ever get sick. Mother Nature takes good care of me. I do have supplies, and clothes for all kinds of weather stashed all over. Usually I on a day like this I don't hike this far from a dry place. I thought since you had a poncho we be all right." He tried to change the subject, "I do really like your red hair."

"Thanks," Anna smiled "but it won't work, I'm still concerned about you."

He stood up and let the sleeping bag fall from his back. "See no more shaking."

It was her turn to give him the once over, standing there in just his shorts. "Ok I don't see any scars and you do look healthy. So what do we do now? The rain doesn't look like it's going to stop for awhile."

"Let's eat something and think about it some more."

"Good idea and good sign that you're feeling better than you looked a little while ago."

"It makes me wonder what I look like most of the time because I wasn't feeling bad, just cold."

Anna motioned for Joe to sit back down then covered his back. She pulled a stool around in front of him and sat down on it. And then she leaned forward an studied his face. "Let's talk for a bit, before we eat."

"Ut oh, and it hasn't even been two full days yet."

"I like you, I like you a lot and I know we just met and I imposed in your terrain but I'm glad I did. You're much more than I expected. I was determined to live out here if I never found you. There shouldn't be any awkwardness between us, because I know we share the love of Nature."

A slight smile on his face, "So you're not trying to tell me you've had enough already."

"Absolutely not." She leaned forward and gave him a quick kiss on the lips. "I was afraid I was becoming a nuisance already. I haven't had many relationships with men but when I did, they didn't turn out so well. They all said they couldn't understand me because they had no interest in birds and animals. There was one guy Richard, he seemed interested but wanted more than I was willing to give. Needless to say the breakup turned nasty. He told me he would find me and I would regret it. I'm only telling you all this so we don't have any secrets."

It was his turn to lean forward and return her kiss. He leaned back with a big smile and said "honesty is one of the best ways to bond. I'm glad I came out here when I did with no entanglements. And I'm also glad you found me, you're different alright but in a good way."

"Let's have lunch." He said as he stood and put on his damp jeans.

"I've never felt comfortable eating without pants."

That made her really laugh, and he enjoyed that.

Later they decided to push on for the rain had changed to mist and though everything was wet they were entering a section of forest with tall trees and little underbrush. The walking became easier and they arrived at Joe's cabin before nightfall.

It was similar to the one by Rock Pond but this one had a small stream out front instead of pond. The bedroom only had one bed, the other room a fireplace, table and one chair. A few cupboards and a shelve with some clothes on it finished the décor.

"I know it's not much but the bed is yours, I'll sleep out here and keep an eye on the fire, and at least it's clean and dry."

"It's just fine; I can tell you were not expecting company."

Joe laughed "The chair is yours I'll use the floor."

"No, we share." She countered with a shy smile.

"Wait I'll be right back." He returned a minute later rolling a small log. Joe set it on end and sat down on it.

"I wasn't talking about the one chair, I meant the bed. I trust you and we will share, I insist." And then she added, "I know you're shy and so am I, so we won't be naked."

Later that night after supper Joe brought the chair and stump outside by the front door. They sat and listened to the night sounds. The clouds were beginning thin and a half moon gave them all the light they needed. An owl hooted nearby and they could hear the wildlife moving nearby, crickets' chirped, the sound of water bubbling from the stream almost put the pair to sleep.

"It's so peaceful." She whispered

"I can leave the windows open if we don't use a light." He said. "Then we can hear this inside."

"Let's do it."

He let her get into bed first while he undressed in the other room. In his shorts he went into the bedroom to find her in a tee-shirt and panties. She waited for him to climb in then pulled up the unzipped sleeping bag. She had taken some of his folded clothes to use as a pillow and left that for him.

"This won't due, the pillow is for you. I'll use the clothes. I can't have you messing up that beautiful red hair."

She made a little giggling sound and switched like he asked.

Joe laid there on his back quietly thinking how strange it was to have this woman in bed with him. She turned and faced him and said, "Lift your head." She pushed part of the pillow under him and whispered "share remember."

He lay on his back a moment longer, and then turned to face her. Their faces just inches apart.

"I think I'm falling in love." He whispered. "Not like in the movies where two people meet and an hour later their having sex in a doorway somewhere. I mean you really make me feel good having you near."

"You talk too much." She kissed him and said "Get some sleep. By the way I think I might be falling in love too."

They both succumbed to the night sounds and fell asleep.

Early the next morning, Anna woke to the smell of coffee and bacon. She dressed and found the table set with two cups and plates. Joe was at the fire cooking eggs. He was fully dressed in jeans and a light blue shirt.

"And a good morning to you sleepy head."

"What time is it?"

"Don't really know no watch or clocks. But it's time for breakfast."

She looked outside and saw sunrise through the trees.

"I was going to let you sleep and bring you breakfast in bed. Then I realized I don't have a tray. Besides I don't want to spoil you."

Anna gave him a serious smile "Thank you for keeping your promise last night."

"What promise?"

"To be a gentleman."

"Then I'll have to admit it was more difficult than I thought, you temptress."

They both laughed at that.

A couple of hours later found them walking under a clear blue sky deeper in the forest close to where Joe wanted to be. Now they both were carrying packs and Anna knew they wouldn't be going back to the cabin. The terrain was getting rougher and Joe stopped, "Let's take a break and catch our breath." After they had been sitting for a few minutes he asked; "what are we doing?"

"We're climbing a mountain and taking a rest."

"Right, but what are we doing?" he repeated.

"Oh I got you; we're getting to know one another, I hope."

Joe thought for a moment with a slight frown. "I've been alone for so long I been content to just wander and explore. It's been enough, now there's so much I want you to see but after you've seen it all; what then? Do we just continue to wander in happiness out here? I admit until you came long I never gave it much thought."

"If you're asking about purpose or goals I don't have an answer yet. You have been out here living my dream; I've only been at it for a short time." Then she smiled, "Give a girl a chance to think about it for a bit. We'll figure it out together, how's that?"

"There is one more thing I should add." He smiled, "I don't think I could live anywhere but out here. The town I grew up in has changed so much since my youth that I don't recognize it. I don't mean the physical place, the people are different. It's all gossip and politics and back stabbing, everyone needs to know anyone else's business."

"I believe you because it's one of the reasons I'm considered antisocial."

Joe laughed, "That's why we're meant for each other." Then she began to laugh with him.

Chapter Three

The town they were talking about was Long Lake and little did they know they were being talked about at the same time. Stories of Anna who was considered odd and how she just disappeared one day. The boy Richard, who had nothing nice to say about her. And then the story of how she ran off or was taken by the hermit who was said to live nearby. The stories grew and someone decided it should be reported to local authorities. Rumors became facts and the Sheriff's dept. had no choice but to investigate. They sent a couple of deputies out with a warden and a ranger to find the hermit.

Within a week their futile efforts brought outrage from Richard and some towns' people. Most didn't care because it was just another story and unless it was important to them, it didn't matter. However, in a matter of days a manhunt was being organized. It was decided that if he was hiding maybe he did take Anna. A larger amount of manpower would be needed to do a thorough search.

They were talking about an extremely large area of thick forest so it was decided to try a plane equipped with heat sensitive cameras. Needless to say that didn't work too many animals. Frustrations grew and the real manhunt was on with about thirty men.

Chapter four

They had slept out under the stars and Joe woke just before sunrise. The sky was beginning to get lighter on the horizon from what he could see through the trees. Something's not right he thought, and then turned to look at Anna. She was still sleeping just a few feet away so he rolled his sleeping bag and began to quietly gather their belongings. Why he felt the need to move quickly he didn't know, but when he was finished he sat next to Anna. "Good morning beautiful," he whispered.

She stirred and turned over to look up at him. "You're dressed? What's going on?" Then she realized their camp was packed. "No coffee?" she asked sitting up quickly. "Something is going on; your expression tells me I'm right." She began to get dressed as he tried to explain.

"Listen. It's way too quiet, no birds or wild life moving. Something strange is going on but I have no idea what."

"I agree and think we should move from here."

They hadn't gone far when they heard distant calls. "My God," Anna said softly "they're calling me." Faintly Joe could hear the calls coming from many different places.

"Why?" she asked. "There's nobody to care about me, so why are so many people out here looking for me?"

As the calls came closer, Joe asked what she wanted to do.

"I'm torn. Curiosity and the urge to run. Believe me I have no idea what this all about, but I don't think I want to know. Let's retreat and hide."

He agreed and they began to run and within minutes found a small cavern almost covered with forest debris. Joe crawled in and appeared seconds later. "It will do, hand me our stuff." He put it inside and crawled out. Get in, it will be ok and I'll be right there. He spread the debris to cover their signs then piled it by the entrance. He crawled inside and covered the entrance. It was cramped but they managed to twist around and lie facing the covered opening. "Let's hope they don't have dogs." He whispered. "I didn't hear any before." She answered.

Then they heard it, a loud humming buzz, and it was coming closer. "Drone." She said so softly. "It explains a lot. That son of a bitch."

He motioned for her to be silent.

Voices close by and he was trying to hear what they were talking about. The drone lifted and moved on which let him hear nearby. "At least we know their together." Someone said. "Damn good tracker the other answered." "Yes, but how did he know there were two people at that campfire?"

"Because he's a damn good tracker." Another voice answered. I know because I hired him. Now let's get moving they have got to be close by."

As the voices faded Joe turned to Anna. "You were saying. "Soon as I heard the drone I knew it was Richard. He bragged about it and even used it to spy on me, and that was him talking about hiring a tracker. What is his problem?"

"He sounds obsessed can't say as I blame him."

"Its ridicules I told you about him."

And then the third voice whispered, "You guys can come out now it's safe."

Completely stunned Joe pushed away the debris and crawled out followed by Anna.

A very tall thin black hair man stood beside their hiding place with a big grin. "I'm that damn good tracker. They call me Dan, but my real name is 'Talks to the Wind"

"Why are you helping us?" Anna asked.

"Because Joe here thinks and acts like an Indian. I have seen you many times. Besides that blowhard has lots of money and I get paid by the day, plus I think Anna will make good mate for you. Now you run that way," he pointed back the way they came, "I will lead them forward for awhile before I lose your trail."

"Many thanks from both of us, Talks to the Wind." Joe said and smiled, "I'm sure we will be meeting again."

As they trotted off, Anna said "I didn't even know there were Indians around here."

"I knew but never saw one. I am nervous about that drone though that's a new thing to me."

"Don't be, it has a limited range from the one flying it. However, where do we go now?"

"I know a place where we can be safe for awhile anyway. We will have to be careful with our trail from now on. He guided her to a wide slow moving brook with marsh on both sides. "I assume you can swim?"

"Hell of a time to ask, but yes I swim quite well. Do we have too?"

"I'm afraid so, we can't be tracked in water. He tied their belongings in her poncho threw it in the brook and jumped in she followed with a little squeal at the cold water. After awhile he grabbed onto a boulder in the middle of the brook and she joined him seconds later. "You tired already?" she joked.

"Just trying to remember where we can leave the water without leaving a trail. The water splits up ahead and to the left is fast water, not rapids but shallow and it could be rough; if we stay in the calm water to the right it's about another half mile swim."

"To the right then," as she let go of the rock and started ahead of him. He caught up to her and they swam more relaxed. When they reached the end of the brook she was startled for it ended in a lake. He stood on the pebbled bottom near shore and asked her to stay right where she was and threw her the poncho. He stepped into the brush and out a moment later dragging a small canoe. Pushing it toward her he held it while she got in then rolled in the back and started paddling. "It's mine I didn't steal it. I didn't say anything about it in case it wasn't there. Now we'll give those guys a run for their money. One more thing, you are absolutely stunning when wet."

"You're embarrassing me, am I not stunning all the time?"

"Yes dear." Then they both laughed. "I'm staying close to shore so keep an eye out for downed trees or rock that might be just below the surface; we're only going to that next point of land. As they made the turn she saw more marsh with high reeds and then as they got closer she saw the small stream only a few feet wide. After a few yards they came to the beaver dam above the water was wider. As they climbed up and pulled the canoe over she asked "Aren't we headed back the way we just came?"

'No we're going to the left right up here. I have a decent hidden camp just a little way in." After Joe hid his canoe they followed a game trail through think forest of large pines. He stopped and pointed, "We should be safe here."

Anna looked where he pointed but didn't' see anything.

"On that slope, just under that big leaning tree. She walked closer to where he pointed and still saw nothing that looked like a decent camp.

"Great if you can't see it they never will." He leaned forward and brushed aside some pine needles to expose deep green moss. He found something that looked like a tree root and gave it a yank. It was the door to his log home. "Stay here till I get some light going" and he stepped inside. She saw light inside and it began to get brighter, and then Joe was standing at the door bowing, "My lady your castle awaits."

As she stepped inside Anna gasped, "It's so big."

"Oh there's more, first let me close the door, as he did he showed her a short cord hanging next to it. "Once inside we give it a couple of yanks and then don't touch it anymore."

"What is it?"

"It sprinkles more pine needles over the door to keep it hidden. The walls and roof are heavy hemlock and spruce. Sorry about the lack of windows but there are ways to see outside. He showed her the small kitchen and bathroom and the bedroom in back. It had a closed door on one side and she asked about it. "An escape route if needed."

"Who built this?"

"Me, many years ago. It's wonderful in the winter, warm and cozy. Oh and there running water for the toilet and sink. I built it in my hermit days as a hideaway.

"Joe, I'm not comfortable here. It's too confining, it's big and comfortable but it's a glorified cave."
She saw his hurt look and continued, "I'm sorry, it really is a great place just not for me; and your hermit days are gone I hope."

"He tried to smile, "Anna my apology, after the events of this morning I wasn't thinking. We'll go somewhere else. This would probably be the first place Talks to the Wind would look if he's been watching me all this time." Glorified cave, he thought she's right that's exactly what it is.

Chapter Five

Hours later they were paddling slowly along the shoreline. The water was calm and so was conversation until Joe spoke. "If we stay on the water they can't track us but we can be spotted by plane or that drone thing. I think we bought some time by going to my camp; by the way I really am sorry about bringing you there."

"Don't be it gave me some insight as to who you were, and I have to admit it was quite interesting. I just felt trapped in there as ridicules as that sounds. I think it was the no windows."

"We're quite a few miles away from yesterday, let's ignore the search and be as we were when we met."

"You're easy to get along with." She answered.

They hid the canoe and headed into the woods and within twenty minutes of following the path of least resistance were absorbing what nature had intended. They found a sloping glen filled with wild flowers and butterflies and sat down to watch.

"This is why I came here." Anna said. "For all this beauty and peace, it fills me and makes me feel whole."

"Believe me I know exactly what you're talking about. I have spent so many days just sitting and watching in places like this. Your mind takes in details you would miss if you had to be somewhere else. I don't mean like how many kinds of flowers or butterflies you see. I'm talking about the fawn hidden right there." Joe pointed to a spot only a few feet away.

"Oh it's adorable, how did you find it? It blends so well with the grass and flowers."

He laughed quietly I was watching its mama over there. She's been watching us and kept looking at that spot also. Now stay real still, Joe stood up slowly, backed away a few steps and called softly "Come on baby, no one is going to hurt you or your little one. Come on its ok." The doe took a couple of hesitant steps toward them, and then snorted, instantly the fawn jumped and ran to its mother. Amazingly they didn't bound away, but began to nibble at the flowers. She only looked up when Joe moved to sit back with Anna. "It can't get much better than this." He whispered smiling.

A bit later even though they were not bored they decided to move on; then moved slowly to not bother the deer. They climbed higher and brush began to get thicker. Though they were careful Joe knew they were leaving traces of their passing this way. Then he spotted a rocky ridge to their left. "That way." He told her. As they began to walk the ridge he explained "I'm still amazed at how good Talks to the Wind is. I'm trying to just enjoy now, but it's in the back of my head."

"Sooner or later we will deal with that. Let's make it later, much later." She smiled. "I prefer to think that maybe we won't have to at all."

The ridge gave them a high but restricted view of the surrounding forest, but Joe spotted water a small pond down in the low lands opposite they way they came. He pointed it out to Anna and asked if she thought it was a good way to go.

"You're the woodsman and besides I have no clue as to where we are."

He laughed at that, "Neither do I, never been here before but I've been in many new areas and always came out." They trudged through thick wood and would have missed the pond if not for the sound of rushing water. A small waterfall fed the pond. There was no lean-to or cabin just forest. But they decided to make camp near the water. Joe cleared an area for their sleeping bags and built a fire. He tried to keep it from making much smoke by using dry dead wood. After some coffee and provisions they were carrying; they sat back and watched the sun as it dropped behind the mountain. The forest overhead was lit with golden light for a short time. And then it grew darker quickly. Anna put her bag as close as possible to Joe's and climbed in.

"I just had a thought," he said "climb out for a minute." As she did he unzipped his bag and laid it flat, then unzipped hers and laid it on top. In the dark he labored to make the two zippers match. It worked and they had one big sleeping bag.

"Why didn't you think of this before?" she asked as she climbed back in. He joined her without answering. She was facing his side so he faced her and said "thanks for today."

"I didn't do anything that deserves a thank you."

"You were here."

"I should be thanking you." She put her arm on his shoulder. "You make me feel safe and that's a big deal to me."

He leaned closer and gave her a kiss which she returned and said "You're welcome, now listen to nature's music and get a good night's sleep.

"Would you mind if I left my arm on you?"

"I would like that." He answered.

The sound of the waterfall lulled them quickly to slumber. He got up once to add wood to the fire and when he returned to bed she had turned over so he snuggled closer and draped his arm over her waist, and fell back to sleep.

Anna woke in the morning to find him snuggled very close with his arm over her and wondered how and when that happened. She felt his breath on her neck and thought 'that's nice' then realized his head was on her hair. I can't move without waking him. Suddenly she remembered the magic word, "Hey hermit where's the coffee?" she whispered.

Joe stirred then jumped as he realized his position. Quickly he pulled his arm off her waist, turned and sat up. "Sorry I'm so sorry. I didn't mean anything. I added some fuel to the fire last night and when I came back you had turned over and looked so cozy; I just cuddled that's all."

Anna sat up and smiled, they were both still dressed "Please don't apologize, it was nice, I just found I couldn't move without waking you and I really was going to make coffee. Its ok we've been sleeping together and it's normal and natural. If you hadn't noticed, I trust you."

Later as they sipped their coffee, Anna with her big green eyes tearing up, tried to explain, "I've never been with a man before. I'm a virgin, yes at my age too." Joe interrupted "Fantastic." And started to laugh.

"You find this funny?"

"No of course not it's just that so am I. I've never been with a woman or girl before you, I mean you know sex."

Now she laughed at how red his face was.

"I know its 2016 everyone hops in the sack with someone but not hermits."

TALKS TO THE WIND

Anna laughed really loud and it was music in the forest and in his ears. As she went to take a sip of coffee Joe reached over and clicked her cup with his. "Here's to we virgins' losing it someday in the forest." Then they both had a fit of laughter. Gasping Joe said "I bet we scared every animal for miles." And then he added "should we stay here and explore or keep moving?"

Keep moving." Anna replied.

They stayed in the valley and tried to stick to the lowlands as much as possible. They did hear a plane circling but it was far away and they paid no attention to it. "Are we lost?" Anna asked.

"We've been lost since we left the canoe." Joe answered. "But don't worry the sun still comes up in the east and sets in the west. We've been traveling in a pretty straight line and should be coming to Lake Lila within a day or two. Then I'll know the territory.

"I've heard of Lake Lila isn't there some kind of youth camp near there?"

"Yes and lots of summer people but we're going to the other end where nobody goes. There are place to stay if the need comes up. Our provisions are getting low and I have supplies hidden all over that area. Only one worry, Talks to the Wind must know I spend a lot of time there. We'll worry about that when and if it happens. Right now the sun is getting low and we need to find a comfortable spot for the night." He laughed, "In this land of lost virgins."

She smiled but didn't laugh.

"Sorry it was a bad attempt at humor. I'd like to think I'm still a gentleman."

Eventually he found what he was looking for. A mossy knoll surrounded with hardwood trees. As they ate supper a chipmunk and red squirrel approached them from two different directions, Anna threw pieces of crackers to each and was delighted at the way they stuffed their face and ran. Soon the blue jays and other birds showed up for their handouts. Then it began dark and time for sleep. As they climbed into the sleeping bag Anna asked, "No hanky panky right?"

"Right still a gentleman." Joe kissed her and turned over facing away. Within a minute he felt her turn toward him, then her hand on his chest. She pulled herself closer and whispered "I no longer think I love you, I know I love you." He whispered back "I really love you too."

"Soon." Was the last thing she said before falling asleep.

They woke at early sunrise and were soon having coffee. "I'm going to start calling you 'Gentleman Joe' do you like it?"

"Not really."

"It's my way to say thanks without saying it."

"I told you there no reason to say anything; we'll both know when the time comes, I think."

"I'll make it easy for you; I'll just shout I want to get laid."

Joe burst out laughing so fast he almost spewed his coffee. "Ok ok enough, I never expected that to come from you. He tried to finish his coffee but kept stopping to laugh. "Some of the things you come out with just make me love you more if that's possible."

"What a nice thing to say and I love you too." She had a really big smile on her face."

Later that day as they approached the lake he said "We should try to avoid being seen, just in case. We'll stay in the forest till we get to the rocky ledges. There is a gravel road by there and once we cross it I'll be in familiar territory."

They made it without event and soon stood looking beyond the new forest at the old one. Joe shook his head sadly. "How many years it took for all this to grow back."

Then he smiled, "But it did come back and now it begins to blend."

Anna was quiet but nodded in agreement. When they reached the old wood she was amazed at the change. Pristine forest with stands of tall healthy beech crowned the boundary and below them long stretches of green, spotted with daisies and buttercups. Birds sang and small animals darted from one place to another.

"This is beyond doubt the most beautiful place I've ever seen." Anna commented.

"And it goes on for miles. Some of it so far away that I've never explored it. He brought her to a small cabin tucked away beneath some tall evergreens. "And there are many places like this scattered all through here." He didn't show her inside the cabin but continued to walk, "We might come back here tonight. I keep canned goods in or near some of these cabins."

Chapter Six

The shock came when they came to the second place. Joe was about to open the door when the soft voice spoke. "Hello hermit and hello Anna. I think you must be part Indian."

"How did you?" Talks to the Wind stood in the shade only yards away and looked like his surroundings.

"In answer to your question I took a guess. You played good tricks and I lost you on the water. Richard was not happy." Dan smiled, "I told him he could fire me, but I knew he wouldn't. He is obsessed and crazy. Most of the officials have given up on you but he has a crew almost as nuts as he is. Most don't trust me but he throws money around and they listen to him."

Anna looked as though she were about to cry.

"Relax woman, they're many miles from here and they won't find you using me. I told you before, I've watched the hermit here talk with his raccoon and take care of his surroundings like an Indian. I will join them tomorrow and eventually bring them in this general direction but they will not find you. Take good care of this woman and we will laugh around a campfire about this, soon." With that he trotted off.

"A good friend I never even knew I had." Joe was smiling. "What would you like to do with the remainder of this day?"

"Head back to the first cabin you showed me."

They walked slow and watched sky turn pink and blue. The actual sunset was hidden by trees but they enjoyed it none the less.

The cabin wasn't much but they wouldn't have to sleep on the ground. They talked quietly about the day's events and retired early. She wore her tee shirt and he wore his shorts; they lay facing each other smiling. "A pow wow around a campfire sounds good," Joe whispered.

"Get dressed and run!" They heard him shout. They both knew it was Talks to the Wind. Joe was up and pulling up his jeans as was Anna. That's when they heard the gun shots. They were still dazed, for they had just gotten into bed and begun to fall asleep. The gun fire wasn't that close but sounded loud in the quiet night. They grabbed what they could and burst out the door and ran. Finding some thicker cover they stopped to listen. They heard a commotion by the cabin then a whisper from behind them.

"Follow me and try to be quiet." As they put some distance between them and the pursuers, Dan motioned for them to stop. "Never trust a damn white man" he joked.

"That blowhard bought a new drone that flies higher and quiet. Guess he didn't trust me either, because he followed me yesterday, and then tried to shoot me. Sorry about disturbing your sleep but I said if they find you it won't be my fault. Looks like it was, so I owe you. I know a place that should be safe."

It was difficult in the dark but he led them up to higher ground and found what he was looking for. A small cave. "Shelter and a good view when the sun comes up. Nobody is going to sneak up on you here. There's a lantern inside but I would skip a fire for tonight. I'll kept watch nearby." And then he was gone. Anna and Joe didn't sleep much that night. They sat in the back of the cave huddled by the kerosene lamp and dozed on and off. As it became lighter in the cave Joe went to the entrance and found he did have a good view of the valley and surrounding area. Anna joined him, "It's so peaceful and look at the sky it's so blue with those tiny pink clouds."

"It is good to watch the sky; look for little black dot and hide." Talks to the Wind said then muttered "Damn drones."

"What are we going to do about Richard?"

"You lucky squaw to have two bucks for protection." Dan said jokingly. "I could go to the authorities but he may have paid them." He looked at Joe "Too much money can make a man squirrely." He motioned to his head" He looked at Anna still pointing to his head, "Too many apples were missing before he met you. You should have seen that."

"I did but it took me awhile, lack of experience with men."

"Good reason." Was all, Talks to the Wind said. He looked back to Joe, "Everyone calls me Dan, and my Indian name is for family and close friends. Old custom that enemies not find out, that's why I dress and act like you folks."

"It's our honor and our private business." Joe told him.

"Good and now you two will be on your own for a short time; I have a mate to check on. I'm sure she's heard stories about this mess. He winked at Joe, "Do your tricks it will fool them but watch the skies too, Damn drone tricked me."

They took his advice and headed into deeper forest where the drone wouldn't be as effective, as they did Joe asked; "the pale green shirt you wore the other day, do you still have it? Better still, do you have anything dark to wear?"

"Camouflage, yes I think so." She pulled out a pair of dark brown slacks and a hooded dark green sweatshirt.

Joe put on a dark green denim shirt and turned away while she dressed. "We will probably sweat our brains out but it beats getting caught."

"Or we could run naked and blow their minds."

"God, you are so funny even in a situation like this."

"Are we lost again?"

"No the Bog River is just ahead we'll follow it to Round Lake"

They did jump a couple times at the sight of a crow flying low. As they followed the Bog River they constantly searched for cover to dart to if the need arose.

"I hope to shove that damn drone up his arrogant ass some day." Anna said suddenly, "This hood to cover my hair is making me nuts. Sorry that wasn't very lady like."

Joe pulled her under some fir trees and removed the hood. Her head was soaked with sweat. "Honey I'm sorry, leave it off." He brushed the wet hair from her face. "If you're up to it we'll take a dip up ahead where the water is deeper."

They found a curve in the river with trees leaning over it and boulders. Joe looked around and listened and heard nothing but sounds of forest; he stripped his shirt and dove in. Anna removed the heavy hooded sweatshirt and the brown pants and followed his example. "Oh God, this feels wonderful" she said as she resurfaced. "No more complaints about cold water." They swam for awhile, laughed and held each other and swam some more. Finally they had enough and climbed ashore. "Don't put that hoody back on," he said "your hair is much darker while wet. I mean it's less of a red flag."

"Ok but you leave off your shirt."

"Fair enough and how are your feet? I know you're not used to going barefoot."

"Much better now, they did hurt for awhile but they are toughening up."

"So are you." Joe said smiling "It hasn't been exactly what we both thought it was going to be."

"I wouldn't change a thing accept the shooting. I don't like guns."

"That makes two of us."

"Do you think Dan is alright?"

"I think He can take care of himself, he's one smart tricky guy."

Chapter Seven

Rumor and innuendo was running wild in town with two sides emerging. One side calling for calm and clear thinking. The other full of anger calling for action. A third smaller group saying wait we don't know enough, don't judge.

The third group knew Richard for what he was, someone who thought he was better than anyone else, and that his money would get him whatever he wanted. What they didn't know was just how evil his mind worked. He now had a third target. "Damn Indian thinks he can cross me and get away with it. Hell he has to go anyway He's seen too much. The way I'll tell it the hermit killed Anna and I killed the hermit. And the hermit must have killed him too. But they'll never find his corpse. And you two know I mean business so you want money or you want dead.

"We don't give a shit about your personal vendetta we're in it for the money you guaranteed us. Those kinds of funds don't come our way every day."

"And we get to keep the equipment?" The second man added. He was talking about two high powered rifles with scopes.

"What do I care?" Richard said, "I plan to get out of this shithole as soon as this business is finished."

Chapter Eight

They found a lean-to on the shore of Round Lake and decided to spend the night there. It was set back about thirty feet from the water. "If anyone spots us we're just a couple of campers which shouldn't raise suspicion. It will be dark soon but let's skip a fire."

"Whatever you say Joe." Anna was watching the sunset. The sun was gone but the sky was bright orange with grey and pink clouds. "Thank you." She said softly.

"What for?"

"For being here to share this with; So many beautiful sunsets I've seen but no one who enjoyed them with me like you do."

"You're going to make me cry. Everything we've seen together is so much more than it was when I was alone. And I didn't even know it."

She put her arm around him with her hand on his shoulder. "Let's go to bed and listen to the forest." This night they both stripped naked in the dark as if unspoken it was agreed upon. Hours later as they lay holding tightly to one another, Joe whispered "Will you marry me?"

"We are married, isn't this God's true Chapel."

"Till death do us part?" "Till death do us part?" she repeated back.

Early morning Joe woke to the sounds of splashing and found Anna in the lake bathing. He ran and joined her. They swam for awhile then scurried back to the lean-to and got dressed. Joe built a small fire for coffee and they sat there grinning at one another. Later as they got ready to move Anna said, "I'm not going to talk about last night except to say I think my gentleman Joe is gone."

"Replaced by a good man, I hope."

"There is no doubt in my mind."

Again they headed into deeper forest, at a much more leisurely pace. A mile or so later they stopped, sat and leaned back against one of the many giant boulders around. Everything seemed to be cover in moss and ferns and they couldn't see much sky with all overhead foliage.

Joe listened for a minute then whispered "I think that damn good tracker is close by."

"Closer than you think Raccoon talker and a good day to you miss Anna. You both look different but we'll talk about that later. Again I come with bad news. I had to send my wife to her family and get out of town fast. Word is there are three coming for us which is good; they are very dangerous which is bad. We can hide but it doesn't solve the problem. I don't think you two want to spend your days like that. To kill them before they kill us is not an option; not our way."

"What are you saying we should do?" Joe asked.

"We hide Anna, and we trap them one by one and give them to the authorizes."

"No no, I'm not hiding I'm staying with you guys."

"No you go and make like you're still looking for the hermit. That way." Dan pointed. "Maybe two or three days that's all." Joe nodded and she knew it was useless to try and argue with them.

Mid day they spotted the drone and two hours of hiding they spotted the trio but they were too close together to attempt anything.

"We will wait until dark." Dan told Joe. "Stupid white man doesn't even post a sentinel." He whispered as they crept closer.

"Which one do we try to get first?"

"None; too close together, but I have better plan, stay close watch my back but don't follow."

Dan crept into their camp and removed their guns and the drone. Minutes later he and Joe were gone. They stayed close till morning to watch the three men. Joe hid the guns but kept the drone when suddenly shouts of anger and cursing started.

"I think Richard still has a pistol but is probably not good with it."

Dan was right because a minute later he was waving it around cursing the two men with him.

"Three snakes with no teeth." Dan laughed softly. Now we use bait to separate them."

"Bait?"

"We let them see us and we go in two different directions and see who follows who."

"You're joking?"

"You can run like hell, because I've see you in the woods and these guys are slow. We'll meet back here where you buried the guns. Get them really lost first though."

They stood a couple of yards apart and waited to be seen. The men cursed and charged up the hill and Richard fired a couple of shots that went wild.

"See I told you he was no good with a pistol; good luck Hermit." They ran together till the men got closer and then spilt. Joe ran to the left and when he looked back it was Richard following. The other two were after Dan. He zig zaged as he ran because Richard emptied his pistol trying to hit him. While Richard slowed down to reload Joe put more distance between them. Joe thought to himself, it was like playing cops and robbers as a kid but a bit more serious.

Being mid morning with bright sunshine he had to be careful. Twice he thought he had lost Richard and twice Richard almost caught up. His rage wouldn't let him quit.

Then Joe got worried and put more distance between them and started tricks with his trail. Hours later he was sure Richard was no longer following. He circled back and found him sitting with his gun in his lap and muttering to himself. "Good plan, Talks to the Wind." He thought to himself as he snuck away.

When Joe arrived at the meeting place, he was stunned to find the two men tied together with Dan standing just a few feet away.

"Where's Richard?"

"Lost quite a way from here. You didn't ask me to bring him back." He laughed.

"That's ok, you didn't bring any rope." He said smiling. These two begged to get caught one in my snare, the other saw my knife. No guns no guts. They both said they had enough of these cursed woods. Richard can fend for himself, a couple days out here and he'll be ready to come along peacefully also." Dan said. "I'll take these two to town and explain what's really been going on to the authorities. You go find Anna and we'll deal with Richard when I get back."

"Good luck in town, and thank you." He ran off in the direction Anna had taken. It was a half an hour after dark when Joe stopped, and thought how foolish it would be to continue in the darkness. But then he smelled the smoke, faint but it meant a campfire. He headed in the direction that seemed right because the scent was stronger. In a little while he saw the glow ahead and thought maybe it wasn't her. It couldn't be Richard but maybe campers. He crept closer found the fire and recognized her sleeping bag. She was in it and awake watching the fire. He watched for a few minutes then made noise as he approached, stepping on twigs and moving branches. She jumped up fully dressed and faced his direction; then saw him. Anna ran to him with a little squeal of delight, and they embraced for a long time. "God I was so worried about you. I never had to worry about anybody before it's terrible."

"I've missed you so much." Joe said "No more separations I promise." Then he explained the day's events as they sat by her fire.

"Then Richard is still a threat?"

"Not really, he is far from here and I gather not and outdoor person. We'll get him in the next day or so."

"Now that you're here can we lie down and just hold each other for awhile?" And that's what they did. Joe hadn't brought his gear so they rolled her bag to use as a pillow and lay on the forest floor.

"Were you afraid alone out here?"

"I was scared for you that's all. Never thought about me, but I was lonely more lonely than I thought possible. Please Joe don't ever leave me again for any reason." She clung tightly and he could feel her trembling.

"The ex-hermit gives you his word." Soon she was sleeping and soon after so was he.

Chapter Nine

The authorities believed Dan's account of events despite what the two men had to say. They were in the process of sending out a few teams to search for Richard with Dan's help; when two men entered the Sheriff office.

A white haired older man and a younger man that looked a great deal like Richard.

"Where's my brother?" He pointed to Dan. "I want this man locked up until Dick is found."

"On what grounds?"

"He's been helping to hide the truth." He handed the Sheriff his cell phone with a three day old text from Richard.

"He and some whore have been trying to extort money from my boy." The old man said. "We have phone messages about your incompetence and what's been going on."

The Sheriff frowned but made no comment then asked "Where you folks from?"

"North Carolina and we brought our own crew to do what you boys can't seem to accomplish."

"Well that's just fine and dandy but you're way way out of your jurisdiction and it would probably be better just to return home and let us do our job." Then the Sheriff seemed to get angrier and put his hand on the phone that was on his desk. "Up here we don't care much for interference and sure as hell don't put up with threats. I can have the State Police here in minutes and have escorted back down south."

"The old man seemed to soften, "We were just offering our help that's all. No law against looking for a relative."

The sheriff shook his head and told them that he would personally see to it that Richard would be found. "I personally don't care for Richard and second the girl missing is not a whore. Now I don't know how you guys work things down south, but up here a man's word is good till he shows otherwise. Dan here is a good family man and has no reason to lie. He walks out of here and so do you two or do I have to make a phone call?"

Richard's brother started to say something but his farther shut him up with look. "We'll give you a week, no results and we will be back." The old man knew his sons, and didn't want trouble with the State police, not yet anyway.

Anna and Joe were feeling guilty about Richard's plight despite his faults, and decided to try and find him and this time Joe brought rope. Within the first day of searching they did find him at the bottom of a small ravine. He looked twisted and broken.

"Oh no!" Anna exclaimed and Joe told her to stay where she was and he climbed down to Richard. He knew before he got close that Richard was dead. He had been mauled. Some animal had got to him before the fall.

"His gun is up here and what looks like blood," Anna called.

Joe rolled him over and said 'bear' to himself "He's gone." Joe called to Anna, and then started back up. He was almost to the top when he heard Anna. It was soft muted scream of panic. As he got to her he saw the reason. A big black bear was just yards away swaying back and forth. Next to it was a small cub and it was wounded. Shot in a front leg.

Joe stood as tall as he could and put both arms out from his sides and whispered to Anna to move very slowly backward toward the ravine and try to climb part way down

"Don't go to the bottom," He told her. The bear stopped swaying as she moved, then stood on its hind legs as she disappeared over the ledge. It sniffed the air as Joe talked to it. "Its ok mama, your little one is going to be ok." He dropped his arms and began to back away. The bear dropped to all fours and started to sway again. "At least she didn't charge." He said as he joined Anna. "We're going to have to leave him for a bit, give the bear a chance to move on. They are not territorial and like to roam."

"Will she eat him?"

"No, no a Grizzle Bear might but we don't have them up here. She was just defending her cub that's all. I'm sorry about Richard, but if it helps he was gone before the fall."

Anna said nothing but looked sad. Then "Could we have helped the cub?"

"Not really, at least not with her around."

Their mood stayed somber as they made their way back. "Maybe Dan will have some suggestions when he gets back." Anna said quietly. "We have to tell someone and I for one don't want anything to do with the town."

"I understand." Was all he replied, he couldn't get the image of Richard out of his head. It was as though some part of what he enjoyed the most was gone. Not Anna but the mountains.

"Guilt" he said aloud, "I should not have left him alone. I never think about nature's violent side. I've lived out here all these years without conflict."

"It's not your fault, it's mine no his. If he had stayed away, none of this would have occurred."

"I can now understand his obsession with you though."

"It was only because I was something his money couldn't buy plus I don't think he was ever rejected before."

"We shouldn't have just left him there I could have tried to cover him with stones or something but that bear completely un-nerved me. I just wanted to get you away from the whole situation."

"Sit," Anna said suddenly but quietly. He did and she walked behind him placed her hands on his shoulders and began to massage them. "Look around you at what's important. It's still here, and so am I. It's only changed if you let it. The forest still has all its beauty and I love you more than ever. Just be my loving hermit again." She could feel the tension in his neck begin to ease."

"I should be doing this for you."

"You have done more than enough for me today."

She stopped and he stood and stretched and they began walking again feeling a little more relaxed.

Chapter Ten

Dan called his wife to explain what was going on and that he felt it was safe for her to come home. He said he needed a couple of days with his new found friends and then he would return to her.

He had no idea of other plans being made for him.

"I want that Dan fellow, he knows where by boy is and he's going to tell me. And that half-wit Sheriff thinks he can threaten me; he has no idea who he's dealing with. I'll have him retired before he knows what happened."

"Pop, we're in Yankee country your political connections might not want any part of this."

"Son, they do what I whatever I tell them to do. They know I can have them replaced just the Sheriff. Besides, even if they don't like us, they love our money."

As their discussion continued, Dan was already miles away from their reach in the Forest.

"Nature's is telling me a storm is brewing;" Joe said softly as he lay in Anna's arms. She looked at the sky and saw no signs of bad weather.

"It looks to be a splendid day."

"Not that kind of storm. My hermit instinct says we're in for more disturbances. This modern crap is not done with us as foolish as that sounds."

"Maybe that's just a residue of yesterday."

"No, Dan should have returned by now and the forest is more quiet than normal."

Anna sat up and looked closely at him, "You know something you're not telling me."

"No really, I just have this gut feeling that I've learned to listen too."

"What do you think we should do?"

"Sit and have a pow wow." Dan said with a small laugh as he approached from behind them."

"Man are we glad to see you!" Joe said.

"Do you feel better now?"

"Relived yes, better no."

"Do you know where Richard is?" Dan asked.

"Yes, but he's dead, tangled with a bear." Joe saw Anna winch as he said it.

"That is bad." Dan replied then explained the events in town.

"I didn't know he had a brother." Anna frowned.

"Brother like Richard, father is worse, they do not think like us; and they are very angry. We should move from here into deeper mountains." He pulled a map from his pocket. "I will go back for my wife and we will meet here." He pointed to a region in the High Peaks area. It was outside the Hamilton and Franklin County and Joe was not familiar with the area at all.

Before he could say anything they heard the chopper. They ducked for cover and watched as it circled just above the tree tops. It was a small blue and white helicopter with at least three or four people in it.

"How could they get so close so quickly?" Anna asked. Then answered her own question. "The drone, it must be giving off a signal. The one you took off Richard."

Joe took it out of his pack and went to throw it because it was blinking but Dan was quicker. He smashed it between two rocks. "Now we run, follow me." They ran beneath big trees and the chopper didn't follow.

Later they stopped when they could no longer hear the helicopter; to catch their breath.

"Why did you keep that damn thing?" Dan asked.

"I was going to give to Anna so she could return it personally to Richard. I had no idea it could be traced."

"Now I must get my wife quickly. You head where I showed you. We'll find each other somewhere on the trail." With that he turned and ran.

"Now I'm scared, I thought this was all done with." Then she added, "And now I have guilt; if I had stayed away it would have been different. None of this would have affected you."

Joe hugged her, "Stop. My world went upside-down the minute I saw those big beautiful green eyes and of course the red hair." He tried to smile, "We're in this together and it will keep us from getting bored."

"I want bored," she said in a fake whinny voice.

TALKS TO THE WIND

"Ok, let's just start our stroll thru the woods and see what happens." Two hours later she stopped, smiled and said. "I'm not bored yet, and you know why? Because you're here with me." She gave him a quick kiss and skipped away. "You're the first man I ever met with no flaws." She called back, as he began to run after her. When he caught up with her he put her against a tree and gave her a long passionate kiss. Then they stared into each other's eyes without speaking. He took her hand and began to walk again; this time they stayed hand in hand and moved slower.

The wood lands extended in all directions from where they walked, and over everything lay an atmosphere of pristine and vibrant loveliness. It was as if here and in no other place, lived quintessential health, nature's pure gift to ease the soul. Gradually they began to forget the trails of the pass few days and absorb what was around them.

Dusk came before they were even aware that night was close, Joe stopped and pointed to some low brush with moss underneath close to an open patch of trees. "A good place to rest and watch the stars," he said as he put their packs underneath as pillows and striped to his shorts. He lay on his back and looked at the almost full moon. She joined him completely naked and said "This moss feels really good, and look at all the stars. I don't think I've ever seen so many."

He turned and looked at her naked in the soft moonlight, he saw small Goosebumps all over her. "God, she is so beautiful" he thought then asked if she was cold.

"No, and you won't be either if you remove those shorts."

Later they did lie on their backs and watched the sky as the world around them became quiet, with just the sound of a gentle breeze. Soon they faced one another wrapped their arms around and fell into a deep and blissful sleep.

Chapter Eleven

Morning came with the promise of another great day, with blue skies and small white puffy clouds. Joe made a very small fire, just big enough to heat some water for their coffee.

Anna smiled as she got dressed, "Maybe we should go naked today."

"I love the idea, but I'm afraid we wouldn't get very far." They both laughed.

"Are we lost again?"

"I'm afraid so, but who cares?"

"Not me," she replied.

After their coffee and a snack they started walking again still hand in hand. "We should still avoid open areas and stick to the trees." In one open area he stopped Anna and pointed to a really high mountain. "That's White Face, up past Lake Placid."

"I've been there once on a school trip. Is that where we're going?"

"Maybe a little past there."

"Lord, Joe that's a long long hike."

"We're both in excellent shape so I'm not worried."

Secretly they were both hoping Talks to the Wind would show up soon. Though he didn't show it, Joe was a little nervous about being in unfamiliar territory. Eventually, they stopped to rest again and Anna asked if they were really doing the right thing.

"We haven't done anything wrong, so why are we the ones running? I know his family sounds a little crazy but if we sat down and explained maybe they would understand."

"If Richard was an example of his family's way of thinking; then we're doing the right thing. I also understand what you're saying. I'd love to go back to where we were before people came calling your name." He stopped talking for a moment and looked at Anna closely. "I said before, we're in this together equally so whatever you decide, that's what we will do."

"Joe, I'm afraid of his family and I don't even know them. But what if we're all wrong about this and it's all been exaggerated in our heads. Besides I don't want to spend my life with you always looking over a shoulder for something that probably won't happen. Please tell me if you think I'm wrong."

"That's our problem; we really have no way to know. I do like your way of thinking, face a problem head on; that's what I've always tried to do."

Anna frowned, "Let's go back; with you by me it will be ok. I'm sure of it."

"And Dan will find us I'm sure of that; like Richard said, 'Damn good tracker'."

They started back at a much slower pace; neither in a real hurry for confrontations. Nature once again began to calm their worries as they stopped occasionally to watch small woodland animals like deer and fox even a ground hog. They continually held hands on their trek. They did get startled by one animal they both forgot about, a skunk. He turned lifted its tail and they ran, not quiet fast enough. They didn't get the full dose, but enough to not hold hands for awhile.

"My God that's potent." She laughed.

"It's not going to be that easy to get rid of. I know you have some toiletries, some soap and shampoo; it will have to do if we find some water."

A short while later, they heard what they were looking for a stream about four foot wide with some pools deep enough to sit in. They stripped and threw their clothes in the water. Anna put shampoo on the cloths and a rock to keep them from floating away.

TALKS TO THE WIND

When they were through bathing and dressed in fresh clothes; Anna laughed, "Well that was certainly a new experience for me. What do we do with these? She held up their wet still smelly ones. The shampoo didn't help much, they're better but I don't think I want to ever wear them again."

He took the bundle and put it back in the stream and then placed several rocks to hold it down. Once it was completely covered he stood and smiled, "That's the first time I ever littered, I think. However we both smell much better." He took her hand again and they started walking.

Now they were more cautious and walked even slower than before.

Three hours later they stopped to rest and eat and disgust how to handle the situation back in town.

"I still hoping to run into Dan and get more information of what's been going on. As you guessed, I've lived a pretty sheltered life till recently."

"How close are we to getting back?"

"Another day, maybe two."

"Can we go back to where we met, before we head into town?"

"Sure, I think that would be nice. It's not much of a detour."

It was a good decision because they were almost there when they heard him.

"You're headed the wrong way, hermit." He nodded to Anna. Beside him stood a tall dark haired woman, she was attractive and smiled at Anna.

"I am called Gayle; Dan didn't expect to find you here. He said you would be many miles north in the high peaks."

'Gale, like a strong wind' Anna thought to herself.

"No, Gayle spelled with a y." she said still smiling.

"How did you . . . ?" Anna asked.

"Dan is a Shaman, I can't see your thoughts however I can see his. I'm part Indian but just a local girl that got lucky like you. I came into the forest many years ago to find peace and I found Dan."

"If we're going to talk, let's find deeper cover." Dan suggested as he pointed to taller trees.

Soon they were sitting in a circle as Joe explained his and Anna's change in plans.

"Being a spiritual man I understand why you came back here, but it is a big mistake." Dan said frowning. "These men think like Richard times ten. They already tried to remove obstacles like the Sheriff. It didn't work and now there are more determined to get us their way. Their power comes from wealth, ours comes from the forest; it will keep us hidden while we plan our next move."

"So do we head back toward the high peaks?"

"No, if we stay together, we should stay more local. We both know this area better than anyone." Dan answered. "Also if by chance we are spotted, we should scatter and meet at certain agreed destination."

Joe nodded in agreement; "I have a place that might work."

"Your underground camp?" Dan asked. "It would be too confining. We should stay outdoors where we can know more of what's going on."

Chapter Twelve

A few days later the authorities found Richard's body and returned it to town for his family. It was ruled accidental but did little to ease tensions between his families and the Sheriff's dept.

They blamed the hermit for the tragedy; if he didn't exist, Richard would not have been in the woods. And they blamed Dan for luring him into the woods with false intentions.

Despite the Sheriff's reassurance that he would continue to search for the missing people, Richard's father and brother promised to return after they returned Richard to his home for burial. There were still a few towns' folk that wondered if the hermit did take Anna against her will. The search did continue but less intensified except down south where Richard's father and brother hired the best they could find and promised plenty of money for the deaths of the three fugitives. They also promised the search would be completely by air, no people on the ground. The father informed the crew he had four choppers in Vermont just outside the Adirondack Park and permission to sightsee over the area. Each chopper could hold six people including the pilot.

Within days the two couples heard the low flying aircraft, hid and watched. They were stunned at the numbers. They expected one or two but six made them every nervous. Four were blue and white while the other two were bigger and darker green. They looked like military with guns on each side with open doors. One came close enough that Joe could see the men inside. What he didn't know was that others had seen the choppers and it was reported back to the Sherriff. He in turn started an investigation as to where they came from. He was pretty sure he knew who they were and what they were after. He called the State Police and asked for help.

The two couples were spotted and scattered as agreed and within seconds Joe knew he was the target as bullets rained down thru the trees all around him. He knew it was impossible to hide as he stumbled and ducked behind rocks and trees. The gunfire stopped for a minute and he heard more off in the direction Anna had run. Anger rose and he bolted away from shelter toward the sound of distant shots. Debris fell around him as gun fire erupted overhead; one shot hit his lower arm and seconds later a second his calf and he went down. He rolled toward a moss covered downed tree and lay still faced down. His leg and arm throbbed but he lay motionless as he heard silence except for the sound the chopper overhead.

In the chopper someone called, "Did you get him?"

"Yah, He's all blood-spattered."

"Give him a head shot and let's get the other three."

That's all Joe heard before his world went dark.

As he regained awareness it was still darkness that greeted him. He could see nothing, but he felt around himself and knew he was no longer on the forest floor.

"Lie still." A soft voice said. "I'll get some light." A candle was lit, and then a second and third candle and he realized he was surrounded by rock except for one wall with a dark blanket hanging on it. He saw that his leg and arm had been tended too and his head was also bandaged. It hurt like hell and he couldn't think clearly. "What's happening? Where am I?"

"Safe, for now anyway." The quiet voice said from behind him. "You're the one they call the hermit." She continued as she walked to his side so he could see her.

She was slender and tall and dressed in dark green slacks and shirt. As she knelt next to him he tried to see her face in the pale candle light. She had snow white hair flowing over her shoulders and dark weathered features with large clear blue eyes.

"Who are you?" He stammered.

"I have no name any more; there is no need for one out here. I exist and that is enough. You were the hermit with no name until recently, so you should understand."

Joe stared and said nothing, and then felt his head, and thanked her for helping him.

"Your friends are safe; they escaped the commotion of three days ago and now are trying to find you."

"Three days?"

"You have a nasty head wound; the other gunshot wounds were minor. No real damage to bone or anything. The one over your ear however cracked your skull. You were very lucky. I didn't know if you would recover or not but I stitched it best as I could, you'll probably have a wicked scar." She reached behind herself and handed him a small wooden bowl filled with nuts and berries. "Try to eat something and see if you can keep it down. I'm still concerned about a concussion. You did get some fluids down while you were semi-conscious; I thought that was a good sign."

She stood and walked to where the blanket hung on the wall. Lifting one side she peered out and then pulled the blanket down exposing the cave entrance which was low and narrow. It was covered with branches and debris but light and fresh air came in.

"It's cloudy and looks like rain coming which should keep the helicopters away. For what it's worth I haven't seen or heard them since they shot you."

Joe continued to nibble on the nuts and berries while his mind raced with confused thoughts. He had so many questions.

Chapter Thirteen

Talks to the Wind found the spot where the hermit had been shot. "Too much blood." He whispered. Anna was frantic with anger and worry. "But where the hell is he?" She almost screamed; "If he's hurt that bad where could he go?"

Dan looked at his wife, "He had help." He said softly. "Someone picked him up and carried him." He pointed to some tracks. "A female in bare feet; see." They looked at the foot prints in the soft ground.

"A woman? But who and how did she . . .?"

"It wasn't from the choppers because none of them landed." Again he looked at Gayle; "The spirit of the forest." He whispered.

"The what?" Anna gasped.

"Come, she went this way." He answered as he started to trot while looking for more signs.

"What, or should I say who, is he talking about?" Anna asked Gayle.

"A spirit as some would say. A woman who cares for this place. She has not been seen for many years; but stories abound of her protection of this forest. If she exists then Joe will have a chance; if not then I don't know what to tell you. Dan believes the tales are true though he never explained to me why. He said he could sense her from time to time and because he's a shaman I trust his conclusions."

Dan stopped suddenly and began to look around carefully. "The signs are gone." He said quietly. He dropped to one knee and looked close at the area they stood in. "This is good; she left signs so we would know he is being cared for. Now she no longer wants us to follow."

"But we can't just give up!" Anna protested.

Dan stood and went to Anna. "Look around at the terrain; they were here and now they are not. I found you and Joe under a rock after everyone else walked by; remember I'm a damn good tracker."

Anna looked around; the pristine beauty of her surroundings was gone, replaced with just woods. Downed trees and forest and quietness; no birds or signs of life. She collapsed and put her hands over her face and began to sob.

"I love him." She said between sobs, "I love him so very much. He can't be gone." Suddenly she stopped crying, dropped her hands and stared at the forest floor in front of her. Anna's eyes widened as she heard the light delicate voice in her head. 'Your hermit will be fine; he needs to recuperate, and will return to you soon enough.'

Talks to the Wind smiled, "You are gifted; she has spoken to you."

"How did you know?" She returned his smile.

"I can feel her presence; she is nearby."

And then; she was there, standing on the embankment across from them. "Your love is strong." She said to Anna; "It is the type of love that surpasses understanding." She looked at the two standing with Anna, "I am real." She said, "Not some mystical spirit, or vision. I help when I can, and those who pursued you are gone for awhile."

"I need to see him, please." Anna begged.

The woman stood quiet for a long moment, deep in thought. "He's had a bad head wound, and needs rest, but come with me." She turned and began to climb the embankment as they hurried to follow her. "I could only cover my tracks for a short distance because Joe needed a great deal of attention. He did not wake up until this morning and I told him you were all safe."

She stopped by some huge moss covered boulders, then stepped between two. She removed branches covering the entrance and stepped inside. Anna was right behind her and spotted Joe lying on a sleeping bag in the back of the small cave. He was not covered and she saw his right leg was wrapped just below his knee, and his right arm just below his elbow. His head was totally covered from over his eyebrows to the base of his skull. His face was swollen and discolored.

He attempted a smile as soon as he saw Anna. She ran and knelt beside him and then leaned over to give him a kiss.

"You have done extremely well, Spirit of the forest." Dan said as he and Gayle stepped into the small space.

"Perhaps you could speed the healing process with your medical knowledge." She suggested.

"You know much beyond my understanding and from the looks of things there is not anything more I could do."

"Uniting those two will do more than you or I could together." She said nodding toward where Joe and Anna now lay wrapped together. Anna had put her head on his chest and he draped his left arm over her shoulder, and they were both sound asleep. "I am needed elsewhere so I must leave here; perhaps we might meet each other again."

Dan and Gayle stood outside the entrance and spoke in whispers.

"She must be in her seventies or more, yet she carried him almost a mile. How is that possible? You saw her, she is real, not a spirit as I thought." Dan asked.

"Her face showed age but her body looked younger and stronger than her features. She climbed up here with no effort; and she was gone when we stepped out here only minutes after she left. Then consider the years of rumors about her; perhaps that is what restricts our thought."

Chapter Fourteen

When the helicopters land in Vermont the authorities were there waiting. The pilots, Richards's father and brother, and the man who shot the hermit; were arrested on various charges. A new search was ordered back in New York State. With the help of one of the pilots they thought they knew the location of the shooting. This search was for the hermits' body for evidence of murder.

Within two days they had found the scene of the incident and called for electronic equipment to help process all the evidence. Trees were torn up and shell casing were everywhere; they thought they had found blood, but were waiting to see if it was human or animal.

No one seemed to realize they were trampling any signs of someone helping him; and within an hour it was determined that the blood found was human and the amount found told them he was most likely dead. But where was the body? As they searched a wider area around the crime scene; they found evidence of three other people who were probably there. That's when the idea of Talks to the Wind might have taken the body, came into play.

The why would he do that; made no sense but the search for him and the missing girl would have to continue. A few phone calls and it was discovered that Talks to the Wind's wife was also missing. It was determined she was the third party at the scene.

Chapter Fifteen

Dan had heard the commotion, left the two women to care for Joe, and went to investigate. He hadn't gone far before noticing there were drones in the air; many drones. These were not like the ones that Richard had; these were bigger and quieter. And then he spotted a forest ranger with a state cop and soon more men walking in a line only yards apart. They were headed in his direction so he slipped back down from where he was watching and headed away from the way he came. He would have to circle around, cover his tracks, and approach the cave from the opposite direction.

He was almost to the entrance when he sensed he was being watched so he stood very still and looked around.

"Damn!" he muttered as he saw the drone. It was high up and hovered just above the area. He knew it had found him, so he went near the cave; "Stay inside and be very quiet" he called. Then he began to run and knew for sure he was spotted because the drone dropped down lower and was following him.

"Damn technology!" He muttered to himself. He knew he could outrun and lose the men, but this damn thing could stay right with him. It slowed and began to go higher and he realized, "range" it had a limited range from who was controlling it. So Dan ran faster until he could no long see it, and then stopped. He knew the men would converge on the spot he was last seen, and that was far from the cave.

Talks to the Wind began to smile then chuckled aloud. "If those folks had brought dogs instead of those flying machines; we'd all be caught by now."

Gayle had heard her spouse's warning then she hung the blanket over the entrance and they sat in the dark and listened. Faintly voices could be heard but none came close to where they were hiding. After awhile they decided it was safe to drop the blanket and let in fresh air and some light.

Gayle got her husband's medical pouch and went to where Joe was sitting up. "Let's have another look."

"My arm is much better, and the leg is getting there; but my head is a whole different story. It hurts like hell, the headaches better but it feels like there's a hot poker stuck in my ear."

Anna unwrapped his arm; "It certainly looks much better; I think we should leave it uncovered and let the air get to it." She unwrapped his leg. "This looks like you'll be running next week."

"I hope not; I don't want any more running or hiding, and definitely no more shooting."

A look of anger passed quickly across her face replaced with a smile; "Back to the days of deer and flowers and butterflies and birds. Sure sounds good to me."

She winched as the last bandage was removed from his head. The gash was deep but it was stitched well and not bleeding, but it looked infected. The hairs around the gash had been shaved, but were growing back into the stitches.

"It has to be opened and cleaned." Gayle said. "I can do it, but it's going to hurt."

"It already hurts really bad, so just do it. It can't be any worse." He tried to smile but tears formed and began to run down his face.

Anna talked softly to him trying in vain to keep him distracted while Gayle cut the stitches.

Soon the wound was cleaned and Gayle produced two long poultices and placed them on the gash which had begun to bleed slightly. "It will draw out the poison. It will take some time, but it should work. I am sorry Joe."

Joe passed out and the two women redressed the wound and let him sleep.

"The poultice will have to be changed every couple of days." She told Anna. "Plus they have to be kept moist."

"Ok, but you'll be here right?" She knew before she asked.

"I have to find Dan. He's been gone too long. I'll leave everything you will need, but I'm worried about all those men. Dan is good, very good in the forest; but these new gadgets these men carry scare him and me. I know you can handle things here and you'll be safe; maybe the white haired women will come back."

After Gayle left, she lit a couple of candles hung the blanket and laid down next to Joe. She put her arm on his chest so she would know if he moved; and fell asleep.

She did wake once or twice when he groaned in his sleep; but she whispered to him and he calmed down.

"It's all been a lousy dream right?" She jumped at the sound of his voice.

"You're awake; how do you feel?"

"Not too good but my head actually feels better than it has for days."

They hugged each other for a long time; content just to be alive and together. She knew he was better when he whispered "Where's the coffee?" She got up and removed the cover from the entrance. The added light and smell of fresh air perked him up more.

"How did I get here? Never mind, you are here and that's enough.

Before Anna could respond; the soft gentle voice came from outside. "I have brought you folks some supplies." The camouflage was removed and she entered leaving the entrance open

"You seem so much better;" she said to Joe, "I knew you were what he needed." She said to Anna. "I brought the coffee you asked for, and again I cannot stay. You will however be safe here, and the Indian and his mate will return within a day or two. The search is now elsewhere but be careful, the drones may return. You four must remain hidden, but only for a short time longer. Nature will protect you as it has been doing. I will explain it this way before I leave.

She, Mother Nature saw your dilemma. That bullet was for the center of your head. A strong gust of wind moved the chopper slightly and a tree limb, to defect the shot. People think you are dead and justice is being served.

There is a purpose behind all of this; which I do not understand yet. Tell the one who talks with the wind, he and I will meet soon." The white haired woman turned and left.

"She was here before, I remember. I don't know who she is or why she is helping us." Joe said.

"She carried you here and took care of you, she kept you alive."

"But that's impossible she's too old."

Dan and Gayle seem to know about her, maybe when they get back we can have that conversation. Right now we need hot water."

Within a very few minutes Anna had a small fire going inside the cave in a back corner. Suddenly she squealed with delight. "The sack she brought, it has yours and my stuff in it; from our back packs. Look Folgers coffee."

Thirty minutes later Joe held a cup in front of himself. "If this doesn't help my head, I'm doomed." He laughed as he took his first sip. "Anna! Lord in Heaven! I really needed this. Thank you thank you."

Anna almost cried, hearing him sound like his old self.

He set the cup down and stared at the entrance. "I'd love to get out there, even if only for a few minutes; but I wouldn't be fast enough to hide if the need came up."

"We can do it." She said suddenly. Anna produced the dark green hat she used to cover her red hair way back when they were running and hiding. She gently slipped it over his bandages; "You're right, the bandages would be spotted from a long way off. Do you think you can walk?"

"Not really, I'm dizzy from just sitting up, but I can crawl." Joe dragged himself to the opening with Anna's help. Moments later she had him propped against one of the moss cover rocks. Then she covered him with the debris from the cave door.

She stood back and smiled, "You're not even there." Anna crawled under the cover, beside him and they looked at their surroundings.

It was cloudy but warm and pleasant. They could hear birds below and a gentle breeze moved things around them; as if to remind them of the old woman's words.

"Do you believe what she said about nature protecting us?"

Joe didn't answer; he had fallen asleep. The effort of getting outside was too much for him.
Soon Anna, with her head on his shoulder joined him in sleep.

Later Joe woke to sunshine and a pounding headache. Most of the clouds had thinned and the sun hurt his eyes.

Anna woke up when he stirred, "Are you alright?"

"Not really, I need to get back inside; my head is going to explode."

She turned him away from the rock, reached under his arm pits and dragged him. He pushed a little with his feet. Minutes later she had him on the sleeping bag, and tried to gently remove the hat covering his bandages.

"God, it hurts." He whimpered.

Anna put a wet cloth on his eyes and began to unwrap his head. The wound looked better than yesterday; it was less red but there was still fresh blood under the poultice. She dripped a little water on them and only wrapped one bandage to keep them in place. Then she removed the cloth from his eyes. He opened them and smiled.

"I'm sorry; I didn't mean to put you thru all that.
It's better now, a little better. Maybe the hat was too tight, or the sunshine; I just don't know. It was so good to be out there with you. I miss the forest." Joe closed his eyes again and slept.

Anna worried as she washed his face, he didn't feel like he had a fever and he wasn't clammy; she left a wet cloth on his forehead, then sat and watched him sleep. The old woman's voice was in her head, reassuring her that he would be fine. 'He needs only rest, plenty of rest. The swelling has to be reduced inside his head. Keep him propped up.'

Chapter Sixteen

"Captain, we spotted the Indian out near the crime scene; but we lost him. Even the drone couldn't keep up with him. He didn't even leave enough signs to follow."

"I've already asked for some canines from the state, And they should be here by morning. Plus I asked for more man power. People are starting to worry about the amount of time all this is taking. Most don't understand the terrain out there."

"I know Captain, it's not the locals. It's the media that's distorting the story. We don't even know if it's a murder or not. We need something from out there. Anyone of those involved so we'll have some kind of conclusion."

The following morning, three dozen men and four dogs headed back to the area where the hermit was shot.

Chapter Seventeen

TALKS TO THE WIND

Dan and Gayle arrived on the ridge in early morning, and Dad asked her to wait by the boulders; because the cave entrance was exposed. As he got closer he saw light wisps of smoke and heard whispered voices from within. He peered inside and motioned for Gayle to join him.

Neither Joe nor Anna was startled as the couple came in.

"You two seem calm and content." Dan said.

"That lady of the forest came back; Joe's had a couple of bad spells yesterday, but it was our fault." As Anna explained what had been happening; Gayle checked Joe's head.

"I think we should change the poultice daily, it might work quicker. It certainly looks better than a couple of days ago."

"The headaches pretty much gone. It's sore but just dull pain, and I'm not dizzy all the time." He laughed, "I need to start moving around but I'm really weak."

"I know of the need to be outside." Dan said as he went and grabbed the blanket used to cover the entrance. He laid it next to Joe; "You girls take his legs I'll get his shoulders."

Within minutes Joe was leaning against a big fir tree in the shade about fifty feet from the cave. His apparent delight from being outside brought smiles to the others. They sat around for a couple of hours discussing pass events and future things to be done; when the voice was heard.

"What a happy group we have here." She was standing only yards away. She came and sat between Anna and Gayle as they stared. "Yes, I am old but not in years but in service to this wonderful forest. And so you will not have to guess, I am seventy-nine." She smiled. "It is just a number. I help the forest and things that live here and it in return helps me with whatever I need. My strength comes from my surroundings." She looked at Joe; "I have seen you since you entered my domain and have watched Dan for many years. You both think as I do in regard to the forest. When Anna came I thought perhaps there were too many people arriving. Natures said take a wait and see approach. I am glad I listened."

She paused for a moment to study the two couples; "Many decades ago I ran away from home and came here with a girl friend. We found a man who had been shot and asked us for help. We refused; but he in return helps us. He showed me things beyond human comprehension and I have followed his example ever since.
He has been gone for many years but I still feel his presence in the forest."

Dan frowned, "What about all these people looking for us?"

"They have brought dogs but had nothing with Joe's or Anna's scent to follow. They did however get into your home and have items of yours and Gayle's. I did however, manage to defect them from here for awhile."

"We'll have to move."

"Not for a couple of days." She pointed down toward the valley; "There is a canoe by the river, take to the water where the dogs can't follow, but be wary of the drones."

She stood and went over to Joe, and placed one hand gently on the side of his head over the wound. "You will make it. Nature has plans for you." And then she turned and began to walk away.

That night they sat together in the cave and made plans. Dan said he would leave in the morning to scout the easiest way to the canoe and also find a good walking stick for Joe.

"Walk? You mean you're not going to carry me?" he joked, "Man I can't wait to walk." Later that night while Dan and Gayle were outside; he asked Anna to help him try to stand. They were successful, but he was very unsteady and needed her support to stay up.

"How's your head?"

"It's ok." He said trying to shift his weight to his injured leg.

"Easy Hermit," Dan said as he entered. "I thought about it and you don't have to walk yet. It's mostly downhill from here so we can roll you to the river." They all laughed at that.

The trek to the river was difficult, but they were soon in the canoe and letting the current carry them down stream. Sounds carry in the forest and they heard the dogs several times off in the distance. The sounds didn't seem to be getting closer but they kept their eyes on the sky. It was clear without a cloud anywhere.

They were coming to an open marsh area where the forest retreated and they were surrounded by tall marsh grass. Without a spoken word, Gayle in the front and Dan in the back started to paddle faster. Joe sat in the middle with Anna right behind him.

Within minutes they were back under a forest covered river with sections of rapids. As Dan maneuvered thru the white water, Joe was absorbing the sound and sight he had been missing; then the sound he didn't hear often Dan swearing.

A drone had spotted them and it came from behind so they didn't know how long it had been there. It meant the controller had to be nearby. They pulled close to shore knowing they couldn't out run it with Joe in the shape he was in. Suddenly it turned and headed back the way it came.

"Maybe it didn't see us." Anna said.

"It saw us, but maybe reached the end of its range. That means they are not close; not yet anyway." Dan answered.

"But they have our location." Joe said quietly.

"If we stay on the water we can put more distance between us, but they will be expecting that."

"And if we head into the forest, I'll slow you down."

"Think like Indian, Hermit; we follow the drone up river. They won't be expecting that. We cut into the forest above them and head in a new direction.

"You're forgetting the white water, Dan" Gayle said. "We won't be able to get through."

"Dan turn the canoe around we'll get as close as we can to the rapids and walk around them. I'm not that crippled."

The sun was getting low in the sky by the time they reached the quiet water by the marsh. Anna had helped Joe while the other couple carried the canoe.

They didn't see any drones nor heard any more of the dogs.

Chapter Eighteen

The Sheriff and the State Police reported to the media that the hermit and missing girl, along with the Indian and his wife; had been spotted and would soon be in custody. Questions about the hermit's demise brought more questions about the murder charges. The biggest question most wanted answered was why they were hiding. And of course what crimes had been committed.

The same questions were being thrown around a campfire by four people under a make shift lean too.

"White man thinks differently." He said with a laugh. "If you show up now, what makes you think someone out there won't try again to kill you." Dan frowned. "Money and anger bad combination."

"You said the Sheriff was a good man," Anna interrupted, "If we went to him and explained everything it would be better than waiting to get caught."

Gayle nodded in agreement.

"How do we do that?"

"We've made it this far; no wait a minute; we need a phone. We make an arrangement to meet on mutual ground; some where away from town."

Joe began to chuckle, "We're all out in the woods, because there are no phones; just us and nature. It might take some time but I'm willing to just walk into the Sheriff's Office talk with him and leave."

"Let's all try to get a good night's sleep and talk about this in the morning." Gayle insisted.

The next morning they sat and watched the sunshine creep down the mountains toward the low lands. The sky was mostly blue with a few wispy white clouds and promised another warm day.

They drank their coffee and had their pow wow. Even though his instincts were against it; Dan agreed they should try for the Sheriff's Office. He knew it would take some time and hoped they would come to their senses long before they arrived.

Chapter Nineteen

Gayle had just finished redressing Joe's head when the voice shouted "Nobody moves! There's nowhere to run this time."

State Police appeared in several places around them, with drawn weapons. Dan frowned but said nothing. They did as instructed. They sat with their coffee and waited while being approached.

Relief came when they saw the Sheriff and some local deputies.

"We were just about ready to try and find you." Joe said.

"Sure you were." One of the deputies answered.

The Sheriff was looking at Joe's wounds. "It looks like they got you pretty bad. Why didn't you come to us sooner?"

"Didn't want to get shot at any more." Joe answered. "We felt safer out here."

The Sheriff told the men to put their guns away and sat with the group. "The men who did this are locked away." He looked at Anna; "Are you here of your own free will?"

"Of course! We just wanted to be left alone to live in the forest. I had no idea of Richards's intentions. Dan and his wife kept us informed of what was going on, so we decided to stay away and hide."

As the story became clear the Sheriff's attitude softened and he radioed for medical help for Joe.

"I'm doing fine. Can't I stay here and come in when I'm ready?"

"Afraid not; you folks have guided us on a merry chase that I don't want repeated. Some in town think you kidnapped Anna and some think you killed her. We'll all go and straighten out this mess. Besides I think you should be checked out by professional medical team; No offence Dan."

An hour and a half later, Joe found himself on a stretcher being carried by two young Troopers. Anna walked beside him holding his hand, when the terrain allowed her. Soon they reached a dirt road where they stopped to rest, and one of the Troopers called for the ambulance to meet them.

The commotion started when they told Anna she couldn't go with him. Joe in turn said he wasn't going unless she stayed with him.

"She can ride with me and I will be right behind you." The Sheriff told them.

Joe stunned them all as he struggled to sit up. "She my wife!" he shouted; "She stays with me."

"Bullshit, you can't be married; if everything you told us is true. How could you be, while you were out here in the woods?"

"I married them;" Dan lied solemnly, "According to Indian customs, recognized by federal law. Look it up."

"Enough!" the Sheriff shouted, "Let her ride in the back with him. I'll take full responsibility."

As the ambulance rumbled down the rough road, Joe whispered to Anna, "That man becomes more of a friend by the minute."

"The Sheriff?"

"Dan; but yes the Sheriff too, he seems fair enough when you consider what he's been dealing with." Then Joe became quiet for a minute or two. "You are my mate; no piece of paper is going to change that. The forest is our Church and we will return; I promise." Then he closed his eyes and became quiet.

After X-rays and blood tests, the doctor's determined Joe was in good health but wanted him to go to a rehab. place to strengthen his leg and arm. Plus keep an eye on his head wound; they had concerns of brain damage due to the trauma from swelling.

"Absolutely not." Was his constant response. And of course that was Anna's as well. She just wanted to go back into the wilderness and pick up where they left off. She didn't like the things people were saying when they thought she couldn't hear them. "Something's never change." She told Joe.

The Sheriff and a deputy showed up about midday to take their written statements of events. The Sheriff smiled, "I thought we'd better do this before you folks decided to disappear again. You do realize you going to have to testify in court next month; against the people who put you in this situation. As a matter of legality," he handed them each a folded letter; "you have been served. "It's just a summons so you have to show up." His smile broadened. "I also OK'd your release against doctor's orders, so you can leave." He frowned, "Don't let us down." And with that he and the deputy left.

Later a nurse came in with his clothes and a wheelchair. "Buzz me when you're ready to leave. I'll take you to the front door. Your friends are waiting downstairs for you."

Dan had an old beat-up jeep waiting outside. "It doesn't look great but it runs well enough. As you might tell, I don't drive it much. Legs better."

The offer was made for them to stay in Dan's home but they said no. Dan drove them near Joe's cabin where it all started. "You sure this is what you folks want?"

"Just a few days of quiet with each other."

"I'll check on you by the end of the week." Dan told them.

They walked slowly trying to absorb their surroundings; but it was not working. "Too much baggage." Anna said suddenly. "It's like we lost something. I can't put it into words."

"I feel it, Anna; the beauty is gone it's just woods."

"Why? It all looks like before."

The voice came from the trees on their left. "It is as it always was; the beauty you seek comes from inside you and how you perceive. Past things have made you forget.

Get some much needed rest and see what the morning brings."

They never saw anyone but they both knew who it was that spoke to them. We will take her advice, because I haven't slept with you for awhile and I really missed that."

The next morning Anna woke, got dressed and went to look outside. She stood at the window amazed. "Joe!" she croaked with her dry throat."Joe come quick, you won't believe this."

He came hopping out in his shorts and looked out the window with her and was stunned; he opened the door and stepped outside with Anna right next to him. They collapsed holding each other and stared at what was in front of them.

The sun was bright for so early and outside was filled with the scent of trees. The forest floor was littered with animals and birds of all sorts; creatures that didn't get along with one another. Ranger came running and sat on Joe's bare leg and chattered to be petted.

"I have never seen or heard of anything like this." Anna said, "Except in Disney movies and that was fantasy"

"You have two more quests" the voice said. It was the black bear and her cub; the cub that was shot. Then the voice continued. "They are all here to thank you for returning home. Most of all, they are here to remind you both of who you really are."

The animals began to disperse except for the chipmunks, squirrels, a few rabbits, and the many kinds of birds. The voice was gone, and Joe stood setting ranger down and went inside to put some clothes on. Anna stood outside a moment longer; spread her arms wide and whispered, "It is we, who should say thank you Mother." With that she retuned inside to help Joe with breakfast.

TALKS TO THE WIND

Chapter Twenty

The reward of the next few days was shear harmony. For Anna and Joe it was like being back to the days when they first met. The forest was quiet and peaceful and very much as it should be. Somehow the tribulations' of past days had been erased. At least until Talks to the Wind showed up as promised, around mid-morning.

"You look much better." He said with a serious expression. "Perhaps you folks should stay here and recover longer. Skip the trial and disappeared." He frowned.

"What's going on? Dan."

"The guy that actually shot you is still in jail for attempted murder. The old man and his son made bail and disappeared."

"You're joking." Anna exclaimed.

"The judge set a really high bail, as if that mattered to that family. They're out and gone, so the Sheriff asked me to let you two know."

"So, what do you suppose we do now?"

"I'd suggest Anna come stay with Gayle and me, and you become the hermit again. But I know that isn't going to happen. Go somewhere new and unexpected."

Joe smiled at that. "You know what they won't expect? Me, to just stay here and wait for them."

Anna just looked at him but said nothing.

"I won't argue with you." Dan said, "But do you really think that's smart?"

"I don't think Richard's father wants any more trouble with the local or State authorities. Maybe he just needs some time to cool off and think clear headed."

"He isn't the type of white man who just gives up."

"Probably not, but we still have some time. We'll just have to let nature protect us for now."

After another half hour of discussion, Dan left with a promised to try and keep them informed.

They wandered toward a ridge of thick firs; mostly balsam, spruce and white pines. As they got closer the fragrance filled their nostrils; and they watched red squirrels and other small mammals scurry around. Birds chirped and sang in the branches over head. The earth beneath the trees was covered in deep green moss with ferns and wild flowers scattered around.

"I'd say our white haired friend has done a pretty good job."

Joe laughed at that, "When I came here I thought I was living alone. Then I find out Talks to the Wind was here with me, without me knowing it. Now I find a woman has been here long before us, without our knowledge. You came along and filled my life; and I was the happiest guy alive and knew nothing else."

"I'm the lucky one." Anna whispered.

"If Richard hadn't entered the picture, we wouldn't know of Dan or our white haired friend; she is a real enigma."

"Do you believe what she said about the wind deflecting the bullet?"

"Yes, because this land is who we are. Some might call us tree huggers." He laughed; "No matter how much mankind bullies Mother Nature, she will take her course. I think she tries to help those who are trying to help her."

"So you think the woman who helped us is Mother Nature?"

"Oh No. but I think that woman is more in tune with her than you and I could possibly imagine. I've always felt safe here and even after what happened I still do. If all this happened somewhere else; I know I would be dead."

Anna looked at him sort of sad, because she knew that was probably true. "Let's go find some water and take a swim."

TALKS TO THE WIND

Within forty five minutes they were in a large pool just beneath a small waterfall. The water was cold but invigorating and they didn't stay very long. Insects buzzed around them as they walked slowly back to their camp. Conversation was light because both their minds were on other matters.

Joe had a traumatized look on his face as he made a little grunting sound seeing the hole in his side; and then he heard the shot as he fell. Anna screamed and was instantly down beside him.

"What the hell? I thought we were done with this crap." He moaned as he waited for the next shot, that never came.

Anna cried when she tried to help. "You're bleeding badly;" She torn off her shirt and tied it around him to slow the loss of blood. "What'll we do?"

"I don't know where the shot came from. Just stay down low and let me try to think. This hurts worse than my head did weeks ago. I don't think I can move."

"I'll kill you myself!" She screamed at the forest. "Show yourself you cowardly son of a bitch."

There was no response, just the extreme silence of the deep woods. The noise of the gunshot had quieted the birds and everything else.

"Try to stay calm honey." Joe whispered, "I think whoever it was, is gone." He passed out.

"Joe please, stay with me; please wake up."

He was unresponsive as she put his head on her lap and sat there crying out of control.

It was not the white haired woman that came to their aid; it was Talks to the Wind. When he checked the wound he told her that the bullet went right thru which was good. "But I can't tell how much damage inside. We're going to have to move him, but very carefully. Just stay as you are and I'll return in just minutes."

She started to protest but he sprinted away and returned moments later carrying a couple of tree limbs and some rope.

Joe groaned and became conscious as they finished making the litter. "This one's bad, Dan; but I'm sure glad you found us. Anna won't have to deal alone."

"We'll get you out of here." Then Dan looked at her "He's not finished yet; he's tougher then he knows."

After they got him on the litter, Anna stood by his feet; not because it was the lighter end but because she was facing him and could watch him while they walked. Dan in the front tried to find the easiest path and told her to try and keep Joe level.

Within twenty minutes they had him on his bed in the cabin, and Dan reluctantly went to get help. He assured them he would be quick.

Anna jumped when the door opened just moments later. It was the white haired woman, slightly out of breath. "I came as quickly as possible, I was very far away." She bent over Joe to check the wound; and she placed her fingers around the area and pressed ever so slightly, asking where it hurt the most.

When she was done, she said; "I'm afraid there is some serious damage to vital organs. You need to be cut open and I cannot do that. I can however ease your pain. The bleeding has slowed and that's a good sign."

Joe tried to manage a grin, "That's because I'm running out of blood."

The woman took a pouch from one of her pockets and put what looked like dust in the palm of her hand. She stood close to his face and told him, "Exhale and trust me." As he did, she blew the dust directly at his mouth and nostrils. He gasped, wide eyed and passed out.

"What did you do?" Anna squeaked.

It will not harm him; he will wake shortly but without pain. You must remain strong for him Anna, I saw what your love did for him before; it will work this time also. However I must go, I have very important matters elsewhere and the Indian returns with help already."

When she left Anna lay next to Joe and began to talk softly, half to herself and half to him even though he was still unconscious. "You promised you would never ever leave me again, remember. You said no matter what we would be together. Please hermit, it hurts so much right now because I don't know what I can do for you."

Suddenly she heard his voice, "Hey sweetheart, don't cry I'm fine, where's our friend?"

"She had to go, but Dan is on his way back with help, she said."

"Boy, whatever she gave me really works. I feel no pain and actually think I could get up." She looked scared.

"I'm not going too; I just meant that's how good it feels with the pain gone."

Anna looked a little relived but still scared. She held his hand and was about say something when Dan and a couple medics burst in the door. Dan was shocked to see Joe was alert and talking.

She waited until the medical folks were with Joe before whispering about their friend showing up.

"Good thinking, to keep that quiet for now."

"I gave him something for the pain, but I don't remember what it was." She answered one of the medic questions.

"He needs a hospital and quick." He responded as a stretcher was wheeled in.

Chapter Twenty One

Hours later she, Dan and Gayle sat in the hospital waiting room while he was in the operating room.

"You know who did this." Dan said to Anna.

"Why didn't he finish the job; he could have killed us both."

"I think the sick bastard wanted to watch you both suffer."

Over three and a half hours passed before a solemn looking Doctor approached them to give an update on Joe's progress.

"He's in ICU and stands a fair chance of recovery. There was extensive damage to his liver which we repaired and he seems to have been in good health prior to this, so the liver will heal itself."

He came and sat opposite Anna; "the bad news is the damage to his back muscles. He may be confined to a wheelchair for an unknown amount of time."

Anna's eyes filled with tears; "No!" she whimpered "You don't understand, that would the death of him."

Gayle put her hand on Anna's arm, "Easy girl, you're right they can't understand him. It's going to be ok. He is alive; let that be enough for now."

"I can let you see him but you can't go into his room."

The trio followed the doctor down a long corridor and stopped by the last room on the left. Looking thru the glass they saw Joe connected to all kinds of equipment. IV's, tubes, and wires everywhere. There was a nurse sitting there watching the monitors; she gave them a thumb up.

It was too much for Anna, she turned and walked away. Gayle found her standing by a window with a blank stare at the outside.

"It looks worse than it is." She said softly.

"It wasn't this bad when he was shot in the head." Anna replied.

"Doctor's are not always right, you know. Dan and I are ready to help with anything you need, you know that. Take comfort that it turned out the way it did."

"I need to be alone and I need to be with Joe when he wakes up. What should I do?"

"Right now he's in good hands and there is nothing you can do for him."

"But if he wakes up, I promised to be right there."

"I think they will keep him sedated for quite awhile. Go get some quiet time; there's a Chapel downstairs perhaps that will help."

"I'm not much of a Church person; I think I'll just step outside for a few minutes. I need the fresh air and hospitals' bother me a lot."

As she stepped out of the hospital entrance she caught the slight smell of the distant trees; an aroma that only someone who lived as she did, would recognize. She found a park bench by some flowers and shrubs away from the entrance and sat down. Occupied with her thoughts she didn't realize someone came at sat at the other end of the bench. It was a woman in jeans and a hooded sweatshirt. 'Odd' she thought to herself, 'to have the hood covering her head;' because the evening was quite warm.

"How is he?" the woman asked softly.

"You!" Anna was stunned.

"Yes Anna, I knew you would come so I waited out here for you. I don't do public; this is only the fourth or fifth time I have ever left the sanctity of the forest. I feel naked no that's wrong, I feel exposed and very uncomfortable. I suppose they gave you good news or you wouldn't be out here."

"He's going to live, but he might be crippled."

"No, they do not have all the answers; that is only an opinion. Return him to the wilderness as soon as possible and you will see what I am talking about."

"Their keeping him sedated."

"I didn't mean now, I meant when he is better. And one more note of interest before I leave; the person who did this has been dealt with. He will not bother you folks again; Nature deals with bullies in her own fashion."

"I don't understand."

"Right now you don't need too, just trust me you are both safe." With that she stood and headed toward the darker part of the parking lot across from where they were sitting. As she disappeared, Gayle and Dan came out the entrance and looked around. Dan nodded toward where Anna stood and she started to walk toward them.

"Are you alright? Honey" Gayle asked.

She made no mention of her visitor, "I'm much better. I guess I just needed the fresh air."

Chapter Twenty Two

Joe recovered quicker than any of them expected, but he was confined to a wheelchair. The damage to his back muscles caused such severe pain it made it impossible to stand. He was offered an operation with no guarantees, and declined. A brace helped with the pain but did little to get him out of the chair.

Dan and Gayle were more than a little concerned with Anna's demand that he be allowed to return to their camp in the forest. Finally Anna told them about her visitor outside the hospital. She had already told Joe and he agreed to return.

Dan's attitude softens a little. "But she's an old lady, Anna. How can she help?"

"Dan, you of all people know this woman." Gayle interjected. "You've spoken of her ever since I've known you."

"I spoke of a spirit, not a real person."

"But you've seen her; she was both;" Gayle insisted. "She has come to our aid when needed, yet we don't understand how she knew."

The discussion went on until Dan pulled over next to the trail by Bear Pond. "At least let us help you get to the cabin.

"We can do it, and we'll need the practice of doing it on our own." She answered.

They knew it was useless to argue so Dan helped get Joe in the chair and hung a backpack of supplies on the back of the chair saying; "It should help with the balance."

"And you have that cell phone I gave you." Gayle added. "If you can't call us, just dial 911 Dan has a scanner and will know if it's you. We'll be by in the next day or two." Reluctantly they drove away.

The terrain was rougher than they remembered, and Joe winced with the bumps. Finally he suggested they stop even though they were only yards off the road. "Are we making a mistake?"

"No." She insisted. "We'll just go slower; do you need a pain pill?"

"No. I can help more with the wheels so you don't have to work so hard."

"This is not work; look around at where we are. We are back where we belong."

"You're absolutely right" he said as he took a long deep breath of wilderness air.

It took a lot longer than either expected but they arrived at the cabin with plenty of daylight left. Joe wheeled himself to watch out the window while she unpacked the supplies

"I guess there won't be any hanky pank." He said with a fake frown on his face."

"Don't you dare talk that way," she smiled. "We have plenty of other things to talk about." Anna pulled a chair around and sat next to him and put a hand in his lap. "No one will understand how much better this is than our other options."

Though they were both looking outside, neither saw anyone approach, so the slight tapping at the door startled them. It opened before they could get to it. In walked their white haired friend. She was dressed in an emerald green outfit that fit her form as though it was painted on. She carried a long staff of some kind of dark wood.

"Now you see me as few have. This is how I dress most of the time; it helps me blend. I have come as promised to share something I learned many, many years ago. A very special person showed me something I thought was totally impossible. Now we shall see if I learned correctly."

She knelt in front of Joe's chair and asked him to lean forward. Then she handed Anna her staff. She placed her hands around Joe and felt his back. "It is here that needs to mend." She closed her eyes and sound came from her that sounded like music. It wasn't a chant; it was sort of a melody without words. She stopped suddenly and reached for the staff; and sat on the floor. A smile on her wrinkled old face.

Joe looked at her stunned; tears formed in his eyes. "Who are you?"

"I am a student of Mother Nature and she has taught me well. My body fails sometimes with the effort of being who I am; however you are young and now whole. Enjoy her gift. Put the chair aside and be happy with one another." It took a great effort for her to stand but as she did she said; "You may not see me again however I'll be watching, for I know Mother Nature has plans for you both."

Anna started to cry as Joe stood and stretched his back.

"I don't know what to say; I was just a hermit that loved the forest."

"Unlike the Indian and his wife, you both belong here. They live in two worlds and they are good people, I watch after them when they are here. Take care of the little bit of pure untouched wilderness that is left. As you have seen it will take care of you." She hugged them both and said, "A final word for your ears only, though you might one day hear more; my name at one time was Susan Butler."

Chapter Twenty Three

They lay in each other's arms that night without much talking, each with so much thankfulness.

When Anna woke that next morning, Joe was standing there with two cups of coffee and a giant smile.

"I really didn't believe anything like this was possible; I woke up this morning expecting it all to be a dream."

"I think we should keep this between us for a little while. I don't want to deceive Dan or Gayle but my gut tells me this is too much information to expose. I feel we would betray Susan somehow." She tried to smile. "It's your decision Joe."

"You know I'll do anything you ask." He pulled out the folded chair, opened it and sat down. "I don't know how long we'll be able to pull this off, but I agree it should be done for awhile."

Toward late afternoon they sat in front of the cabin watching and listening to the birds; and Joe heard Dan approaching. Joe smiled as he realized it was the first time Dan was unable to sneak up on them.

He appeared from the thick brush that bordered the path. "Well you two certainly look better." He sat on the ground in front of them. "How are you making out?"

"Better than I thought we would, I don't like the idea of her having to do so much for me, and she's good about it, but I still feel guilty."

He laughed, "Squaw always takes care of Buck. Buck provide, squaw cook."

"I wonder what Gayle would say if she heard you?" Anna asked.

"She would say stop trying to sound like Indian and he's full of bull." She appeared behind him. "You thought you would leave me behind and visit without telling me."

"I didn't know what I would find, and you worry too much."

"So I should stay home and cook?" She laughed. "You know he was joking right? I must add you both seem better than we expected.

"The familiar surroundings, fresh air, and quiet time together." Joe answered. "We just needed to get back to who we really are."

"What about the pain?" Gayle asked, looking concerned.

"I try not to think about it and I have enough medication to last awhile. The patches they gave me help a lot, but I don't think I'll be running soon." That caused an awkward silence. "But the day will come, I know it; when things will turn around and become normal."

"You set high goals hermit." Dan looked sad, "Slow and easy will get you there."

Anna had remained quiet most of the time since they arrived. "But look how much better he is after returning here, and it's only been a day."

"We only came to see if there was any way we could help; not to reduce your hopes."

"We know that; you are our only friends. Joe I changed my thoughts about what we talked about. They deserve better from us."

Joe grinned from ear to ear; "That's my Anna. Now please listen to the whole story before you judge us."

Anna removed the parts of the chair that held Joe's feet off the ground; and he stood up.

The couple looked at them dumbfounded. "What the hell is going on?" Dan said.

"Our white haired friend came by last night and she fixed my back."

There was dead silence for several moments while those words sank in.

Dan remained quiet when Gayle asked how that was possible.

"She knows things we can't begin to understand." Anna replied. "She touched his back and said something that sounded like music, and then she collapsed, and Joe was better."

Dan said, "Can I please see your back?"

Joe lifted his shirt and turned around, while Dan looked at his healthy muscles. "No scars from the doctors. Why did she not do this when you were shot?"

"I don't know Dan; that's why we weren't going to say anything. We wanted some time to work this all out. I wanted to call it miracle but those come from God."

"Medicine men make what appear to be miracles to those who don't understand; but this is different. She took away what was wrong even the scars. It is like no medicine I have ever seen."

Dan," Gayle interrupted, "You have talked about this spirit ever since I met you. Now you realize the spirit is a real person; is it not possible that she is both? The real essence of Nature."

In an attempt to change the subject Dan asked, "What about the shooter? Aren't you nervous about another attempt?"

"The woman that helped Joe said we were safe and Nature had taken care of him and he couldn't bother us anymore. I didn't ask what she meant, but I believed her."

Joe smiled as he said "I know you guys can find your way home in the dark, but please stay. We make a mean breakfast and excellent coffee." Anna seconded the notion with "Please."

The next morning over coffee; Anna watched them for a moment before asking. "Have you ever heard of the name Susan Butler?"

Dan frowned, "Why are you asking about her? That's been many years ago. Wait! Don't tell me this woman claims to be her."

"Yes."

"Impossible, she died a long time ago. We heard stories of her when I was little. Some said she was a nut case that claimed to see and talk with dead people; and she would tell folks that the devil himself was chasing her. She wrote a book about it and then vanished. She's been forgotten for a hell of a long time. Even the few friends she had said that her mind had left her long before she was declared dead."

Gayle said, "If my memory serves me correctly she would be well over a hundred if still alive. They can't be the same person."

This woman said she was seventy nine remember, back in the cave."

"Why would she claim to be someone she not?" Anna asked.

"She was genuine in my eyes, when we first met her." Dan said. "So I have no answers. Fact is, if you two trust her that's good enough for me; I don't care what name she uses."

"We're going to ask one big favor from you and Gayle." Joe said; "Please keep what has happen between the four of us. My gut tells me it's the right thing to do for now."

Dan laughed, "I understand white man's superstitions. If word gets out, there will be no place for you two to hide."

Chapter Twenty Four

After their friends left, Joe and Anna reached a mutual agreement to move. "There really are few places of untouched forest. Places where no man has walked or seen except from the sky. They are becoming scarce because of logging and rich people buying up acres for get-a-ways."

They spent that day filling back packs with as much supplies as they could carry and that night; wrote a note for Dan and Gayle

It was overcast and humid the next morning as they started their trek. They talked quietly and stopped often to rest and enjoy the solitude.

"Are we there yet?" Anna joked, about mid-day.

"I don't know where, there is."

They stopped for a lunch break by a small brook with a little stream running into it. The stream was only a foot wide, clear with a sandy bottom and very cold. "There's probably a spring nearby." She said.

"You're getting good at this; and you're right there is."

Then suddenly she asked, "Where do you think Susan is?"

He pointed to three fir trees in an open area silhouetted against the sky. "You see the lighter green at the very top; that's this year's new growth; and that my love is where she is. The birds singing, that's her. I don't know where she is because she everywhere."

"You should be a writer of prose."

"Yah right."

A few hours later they came upon what most would call old forest. Thick woods of tall trees; the ones that had fallen were coated with dark green moss. The earth was damp, though no water could be seen or heard. By late afternoon they were struggling to make headway. They climbed over and under deadwood, thru thick brush and tall ferns. Then they climbed upon one of the huge boulders; even that had trees growing from it. Dropping their packs, they laid in the moss to catch their breath while insects buzzed around them. Finally Joe stood and looked at the surrounding terrain; one side sloped south toward what looked like easier going. It also looked like there should be water close by because everyplace else was up.

Eventually they did come across a tiny stream and followed the flow eager to see if it led to a river. It didn't it led them to a marsh and dusk and more insects. They retreated to more solid ground, build a small fire and laid out the sleeping bags.

"A little disappointed?" he asked her.

"No, we're together that's all that matters to me."

"You'll never cease to amaze me. This was a tough day, and not once did I hear you complain."

The smoke from their fire kept the mosquitoes at bay as they climbed into the sleeping bag. As they lay there, Joe asked, "Do you hear that owl?" The muted hoot was close by. "It means it's hunting for mammals; mice chipmunks, that sort of things, not fish.

"So?"

"So there has to be drier forest nearby."

"Get some sleep and stop worrying about where we are."

Over coffee the next morning he smiled, "We're in trouble; the sun shouldn't be coming up over there, it should be over there." He pointed to where he thought east should be.

"Now you admit we're are lost." She smiled back.

"No, just twisted around a little. The sun must have moved while we were asleep."

"They both laughed at themselves. The nearby marsh looked much better than it did in the dark.

"Do you think, if we called for our friend; she would answer?"

"I doubt it. She really is in everything around us; but her physical being I have no idea."

They continued their walk for the next two days and finally arrived at what they thought was untouched forest.

It was early morning with the promise of a bright day. The blue sky was free of clouds and a soft breeze moved things just enough to make them feel welcome.

"It's so beautiful." She whispered. He nodded in agreement as he looked around at their surroundings.

"Now this is as it should be."

The sunshine contained nothing except abundance of beauty. From where they stood in all directions, over everything lay an atmosphere of pristine and vibrate loveliness. Here lived quintessential health; Nature's pure gift to assuage the soul. The effect of their surroundings was a form of substance vivid and delicious.

Tears formed in her eyes. "I thought what we've seen so far was great, but this is beyond description. It's so beyond words; now I know what our white haired friend was talking about."

"I've dreamt of this but never thought of it as real." He replied.

"Can we really stay here? I mean live here."

"Yes."

"I'm afraid only for little while." The voice told them. It came from the gentle breeze and they saw no one; but they recognized her voice.

"Susan, where are you?"

"I am here, I am everywhere. This is my home and you are welcome here. No one has ever been to this place and hopefully never will, with you two being the exception."

Joe looked bewildered; it was as though she whispered to each of them, yet couldn't be seen.

"It's no big mystery, it is this place. Be comfortable and relax, I will join you in a few days."

They found a small meadow and camped there. The only fires they made from dried dead branches. They tried to not disturb anything because it all seemed so sacred.

On their second day; she came as promised. She was dressed in that teal outfit that fit her form like it was painted on. "When you two arrived you looked everywhere for me as I spoke to you." She smiled; "Everywhere but up. I was in the branches of a tree right over you. I don't climb as easily as I once did, but I still enjoy it."

"You mentioned we couldn't stay." Joe said hesitantly.

You have a trail coming up next month; that's only a few weeks away."

"I really didn't plan on showing up. That world out there can do without me; and I've done nothing wrong to answer for."

"If that is the case, then you are welcome to stay and become part of this place. There are far too few places like this left, but I make my rounds and check each and everyone periodically. You two can care for this area while I'm gone."

"But we. . ." Joe started

"You love Nature and Her creatures; you don't interfere, you watch and enjoy. They will come to know you and you two in turn will understand your purpose." She hesitated for a moment; "You only have to co-exist and one day perhaps I can explain further."

She left them that afternoon with the promise to return as soon as she could.

When she was gone; Anna asked "How can we care for this place? We don't even know how much area we're talking about. And care for it how?"

Suddenly it came to him; "Energy." He said loudly. "All life is energy; that's how we're connected."

"Joe, honey; one step at a time, we'll figure it out together. For now let's just enjoy this place we found."

Anna was right, the place was almost magical in the way it made them feel. There were no words to describe the absolute beauty of pure nature. They felt like intruders as they wandered around. That night they lay on the ground and looked at the stars and watched the fireflies dance.

Joe spoke quietly, "This isn't for most people; they would say it is really pretty and remember it for awhile. But they would not grasp what is really here. You and I are unique because we chose this; everyone else would miss their way of life and say we are crazy. Hear the crickets and frogs and other night sounds; that's our music. I never dreamed I would have you to share it with."

"And I would have none of this had I not met you."

Chapter Twenty Five

The soft rain gave the forest a quiet reverent feeling that did not help their moods.

TALKS TO THE WIND

The guilt Talks to the Wind felt was intolerable; as he paced back and forth in front of the cabin. He chanted softly, half to the spirits, and half to himself.

Gayle tried in vain to comfort him. "It was their choice and you could not have stopped them."

"He was in a wheelchair; I should have refused."

"Honey, you saw the looks on their faces; it is what they wanted."

"I am responsible for this, he was a good friend and I let him down."

"No! You did what he asked, that is what a friend does."

"He wanted to meet with the white haired one; she did not come and this is the result."

The doctor came out of the cabin during their conversation.

"Dan, Gayle, as best I can determine, he died of complications from his wounds; she died of a broken heart. I know that doesn't make much sense, but that's certainly what it looks like."

They were discovered in bed, wrapped in each other's arms with a look of utter peace on their faces.

"It looks like they passed the night you folks brought them here; but this was not your fault. Sorry for your loss." The doc. added as he walked up the path towards his car.

Moments later Talks to the Wind, smiled.

"We are still here;" the wind whispered."

"Gayle?" he asked.

"Yes." She answered, "I hear them.

"Do not be sad, you did the right thing and we are grateful; now we will never have to leave this unbelievable place."

Then there was the silence of the deep forest.

The end

TALKS TO THE WIND

TALKS TO THE WIND

Made in the USA
Middletown, DE
15 September 2016